Texas Heat

and Other Stories

SECOND EDITION 2023

Cataloging-in-Publication data is on file with the Library of Congress.

Cover design by Miranda Ramírez

Printed and bound in the United States of America
First Edition Copyright: 2005
Second Edition Copyright: 2023

TRP: The University Press of SHSU
Huntsville, Texas 77341
texasreviewpress.org

Texas Heat
and Other Stories

William Harrison

TRP: The University Press of SHSU
Huntsville, Texas

Table of Contents

ELEVEN BEDS

1

Night on Lake Dallas in the Texas summer: the water gives back starlight and his girlfriend is fifteen years old, freckled, and they await the magic of the moonrise. Over soft grass she spreads out a blanket and the scent of her burns inside it, a delicate soapy ignition. The adults—her parents and their friends—drink out of bottles wrapped in brown paper sacks. Their laughter skims over the waves: signals to other campsites, to other family groups, and to the sexual ache of the evening.

They stand on a rock ledge beside the shore, boy and girl, leaning together, their bare shoulders touching, as the adults unfold and arrange cots. Her father watches them as he sips from his bottle, though, and he knows what the night means. He calls the boy's name—hey, Will, c'mere!—and the invitation is a command. The girl squeezes Will's fingers as he leaves her side. When he's gone the mother comes and places an arm around her daughter, whispering, and the lake whispers back, expectant, and through the giant cottonwood trees on the far shore an orange and lunatic moon hides in the branches.

The father points and says it plainly: if she sleeps over here, then put your cot over there. As they talk their faces are shadowed and the moon rises larger than a fist, so crazy in its hallucination that it drives away the stars.

Later the father drifts off into drunken sleep as the nightbirds catch the moonlight in their frenzy. Over the moondark lake the picnic ground receives the noise of cicadas and the tin music of a distant radio Will searches for the girl's blanket, finding it, at last, in the deep blue shade of the trees, in the cave of its own delirium. He calls out and hears Myla's soft reply.

They wrap themselves in the blanket, in the darkness, and with a single economical movement she's naked for him. Never mind the others, never mind anything, and their rhythms become a single rhythm as she guides him into her small body. Her virginal bloodshed mixes with the dried blood on his shirt, blood of the fish he caught in the afternoon, and suddenly they're experts at this ancient act. He whispers, yes, keep me here, right here, take me and keep me, never let me go, right here in this place, and a voice deep inside her answers, please, yes, take me away, take me to all the places I can never go alone, get me out of here.

2

At a lodge in New Mexico they meet again.

They are students at different colleges on a winter holiday, and he boldly takes a seat across from her in the cafeteria on top the mountain. They both wear rented ski boots and borrowed clothing for the occasion and as he takes his seat, clumsily, he bumps the table and spills a bit of everyone's hot chocolate. Myla's black ski bib shows off her figure and her incandescent freckles part in a smile. His manner is all pretension: a forced laughter, too much talk, a boast that he edits his campus newspaper—a fact she already knows—and an awkward and boyish insouciance. Her girlfriends look on in smirking wonder as he tries to impress them all, but then, suddenly, he says, okay, time for another run, and he casually suggests that Myla go down the slope with him. To the amazement of her friends she quickly arises, fumbles with her mittens, drops them, trips in her silver boots, groans with pleasure, and goes along.

They ski through bright powder for two hundred yards, then pull up, breathlessly. Where can we go?

They enter the dormitory he shares with five other guys where they pull the goosedown coverlets off all the beds, steal all the pillows, and fill up the bathroom with softness. It's the only door they can lock and they cushion the tile floor, the fixtures, and spare only the mirrors so they can become their own audience. Then feverish acrobatics and wild display: the mirrors say, yes, do that, go there, and later they emerge exhausted, a bawdy laughter sealing the old intimacy they've rediscovered.

3

At lunch in the Russian Tea Room they sit in bright leather booths, the New York literati conversing around them—or so Will imagines—as his new agent, his first editor, and his new bride eat out of each other's plates. Hm, try this! Myla insists, and they laugh and stab at morsels of food. His first book, a thin little volume of short stories, adorns the white tablecloth along with the wine glasses and heavy silver, but it is the young bride, not the young author, who wins all the attention. She throws her head back in a deep, genuine, womanly laughter, her eyes flashing, and where did the girl go, he wonders, and who is this? Overdressed matrons at the other tables stare with envy at her freckles and the editor—a Harvard man wearing wide red suspenders and a bow tie—obviously craves to kiss her cleavage, her slender neck, and her laughing mouth.

Afterward they stroll arm in arm, passing the galleries on 57th Street, then at The Plaza in a room paid for by the publisher they argue over flowers. At his own expense Will has filled the room, encircling the bed with bouquets, and his extravagance annoys her although the room swirls with color and the perfume addles their senses. Too much, she scolds him. We might want to travel on our own, spendthrift, big author, and what'll we do for money? You'd better get a job and get an idea for another book, quick, because we can't eat roses, can we?

After this first of their many squabbles over money she sleeps at the far edge of the beflowered mattress.

The next morning at breakfast in the Edwardian Room he tips the waiter too little, she tells him, and with frustration he tosses a spoon into his empty plate.

4

They buy their first dwelling, a four-room cabin beside a Hill Country stream in Texas: a screened porch, an arid magic in the evenings, an old Royal typewriter in the potting shed where he isolates himself to try writing another book. They sleep in the bed with rough tree trunks as its four posters, a corduroy chair beside it where she sits and reads.

Twice each week he lectures at a nearby college, commuting in their only car, an old station wagon, leaving her to stroll beside the narrow creek, to smile among the neighbors, to sew, to hate television, and to prepare his supper. One day she walks up on a coiled rattlesnake and her pulse is still racing when he returns. They watch the night sky through their expensive telescope, learning the constellations as the cosmos wheels around them. Some nights they drive into town for movies and tacos, and month after month she waits, waiting on his talent, patiently hoping, and the book isn't about anything he knows, but his confidence calms her.

Her parents visit, remarking on how poorly the cabin is furnished and appalled by the expensive telescope. Her father, drunk, argues with Will over politics. Later, his mother visits, nervous and apprehensive, and when she finds a scorpion the size of her thumb she bursts into sobs and soon departs.

At the end of each week Myla reads what he has written and believes each line. She doesn't know where it comes from or exactly what it means or who he is, and tells him so. Yet she accepts with her innate practicality all these mysteries because, after all, the editor far away has sent hard cash, and someone else obviously believes, too, so Will can just sit out there in the potting shed with his imagination and his silences. At the same time she's aware that he watches her hands as she peels potatoes at the sink and the slope of her naked shoulders as she sits reading in her bra and panties, so she wonders if he's memorizing her, studying her and committing her to memory because somehow they are going to leave one another.

One night he heaves himself into her open thighs, so that the bed transforms itself into a dark forest where they lose themselves, and as they finish and lie apart, bruised and dreamy, she whispers, there, feel that? Feel what, Will asks, and he thinks of earthquakes or the moon pulling at the tides, and whispers back again, feel what? She sleeps, not answering, yet she knows: he has flowered inside her, she has conceived, and this cabin is suddenly a great castle, its rooms adorned with immense fireplaces in towers of rock, a stone bridge arching over their moat, tapestries hanging on the walls of the great hall, and this is a legacy, this place for all who come afterward, for children and grandchildren, and this is their moment in the silence of the universe, their tiny wheel within the endless wheel, stars surrounding them like fate.

5

From the shuttered windows of their hotel in Venice they gaze out toward a white immensity that the desk clerk insisted was Desdemona's Palace. But Desdemona is a fictional character, Will argued, a creation out of Shakespeare, but, si, yes, scusi, this was her true palace, just there, no extra charge.

The Hotel Flora's wide rooms are furnished with dusty antiques and on the beds in the adjoining room their children sprawl out for afternoon naps, the freckled girl and the twin boys with their mouths open in exhausted sleep. Myla combs out her hair, arms raised before the oval mirror with its peeling frame, her naked breasts pulled high. In motherhood her beauty increases. A carton of Murano glass sits atop the stacked luggage: goblets destined to be lost. From the canals voices float up from the gondolas and the odors riding on the breeze are jasmine and garlic.

She scolds him for spending too much money traveling and argues for settling down, for adding rooms to the house in Texas, for savings accounts, saying, think about the dental bills, how about bicycles, if you hadn't sold that short story we'd be flat broke, what about school clothes, this success won't last. He pulls her down on their bed to silence her with a kiss, and she says, quiet, don't wake the children, shut the door, as he answers, c'mere, open up, there, and they both know the addictive truth: they're sensuous nomads, inebriated with new places, stuck in some time warp of sexual passion with each other, giddy, dragging kids and luggage around in their ardent wake, wanderers, sending postcards from lost temples and exotic ruins in faraway jungles, and this is their only constant, this narcotic pleasure, this wet thrust, this.

6

They travel in Africa with another couple, his old school buddy, a journalist with assignments, and the second wife, a slender child bride with enormous breasts. In their shared suite at the old Norfolk Hotel they run around in their underwear drinking Salty Dogs, hiding in the gun closets, singing, then they hire a driver and a rickety Hertz Land Rover, leave Nairobi, and go up to Treetops. In the cold tiny room of the famous treehouse in the highlands Myla accuses him of paying too much attention to the friend's bride and he laughs, saying, right, I can't get my eyes off those tits of hers, and he somehow laughs too long and too loudly over his confession.

In the middle of the night he gets out of bed and strolls onto the deck overlooking the lighted waterhole. A few other insomniac guests are out there to watch a herd of indolent water buffalo. Somewhere in the night—the suburbs are encroaching—he can hear a boom box. This elaborate tourist stop fails to inspire him, so he leans on the railing conjuring up another Africa, the primeval savannah, distant drums, lost myths.

When his name is softly spoken he turns to find his friend's wife at his side. Myla calls her Bambi. Bambi begins to pay elaborate attention to the water buffalo, to the moonless night, and to his face—wearing, he fears, an expression of goofy romanticism. She draped in a thick gray blanket and opens it to invite him inside. It's warmer in here, she trills, and he sees that she wears only a lace teddy that fails to restrain her heaving chest. They suck in their breaths, both of them incapable of speech as her breasts flatten against his ribs, and then a movement catches their gaze, a great shadow at the dark edge of the waterhole. A big male lion slowly circles that nimbus of spotlights: casual, haughty, watching the warthogs scatter before him as he makes his way toward the herd of buffalo, moving toward them with a regal disdain. Will and Bambi watch mesmerized inside the blanket as their hearts pound together. Other guests accumulate around them to gawk at the lion, but by this time Will and the young wife stare into each other's loony eyes, caught in the spotlight with all the other thirsty and rutting creatures of the night.

Simba, he says stupidly, and her nipples seem to grow erect against his side. Her mouth awaits his kiss.

But then Myla, standing beside them, clears her throat.

The lion springs through the air, bounding off one sleeping buffalo then another, scattering the herd, and with grunts and a roar the night explodes into action.

Minutes later Will's back in that tiny room where Myla stands above him on the bed, screaming. Since the rooms at Treetops are jammed together—one can hear a cough from one room to the next—everyone shares in Myla's rage. You shit, she bellows. Cheater. Fuckhead. When he urges her to quiet down this energizes her. She screams, oh, that goofy look on your face, you were out there playing blanket bingo in front of everybody, rubbing up against those big bazookas of hers, and in the midst of her ranting Myla steps off the bed onto the nightstand, sending a metal washbowl to the floor. Her voice cracks and she begins to weep, and we're in this awful place, I can't even call a taxi, and we're trapped in this dumb marriage, and, oh, the poor children, and he feels trapped, too, for out there in the darkness is the wilderness, nyika, the unmapped and unexplored solitude, the nothingness.

7

A rented house in Hampstead: temporarily settled.

Their newly teenaged daughter cruises London with her girl- friends from the American School, all of them wearing capes, talking Cat Stevens, Harrod's, hamburgers and movies. The pensive son learns the guitar, suffers asthma, rides the tube with his scrawny pal, and talks to Will about writing while his twin brother bounces balls, dribbles balls, strikes balls, and watches televised ballgames. Look, see, I revise over and over, Will says about his writing. They crowd beside each other in the study, their knees touching, his son's peppermint breath on his cheek, a ball being thrown against some wall, and they study a page of film script from a project that will soon bring money and embarrassment: a delicate and somewhat experimental short story of Will's soon to be transformed into an action movie with additional dialogue supplied by the stuntmen.

While Will revises again and again, Myla takes the children to the ballet at Covent Garden, to Windsor Castle, to the orchestra on the Embankment, to paintings by Gainsborough and Constable, to Stonehenge, and by mistake—don't watch this, kids—to the Rocky Horror Show. All of them dine at Simpson's, at Veeraswami's, and at a steamy little Chinese café in the neighborhood. In Highgate Cemetery they stand before the graves of Karl Marx and the inventor of Bovril. Will takes lunches at Pinewood Studio and on Saturdays escapes to a local pub and to Bernard Stone's bookshop in Kensington. Although her fingers ache with arthritis, Myla takes a weekly ceramics class. They stay busy distracting themselves—often from one another. And they sleep in their flannels, adream in goosedown as winter howls around them and as the timbers of the old house creak and sigh.

7

Are we drifting apart? she wants to know.

It's just suburbia, he tells her. And money. And this damned film script.

Every four or five days they fumble into one another's flannels, searching for the old nakedness as the fourposter laments their soft proprieties. They touch with domestic formality, with a sexual courtesy, whispering, yes, please, more of that.

8

He stays in the bungalow down at the end of the walkway at the Bel Air Hotel: a fancy address for the summer, bougainvillea, white swans gliding under the wooden bridge, expenses paid by the studio. He's the California wordsmith, the glib fabricator, yet he can't find the right combination of words to say to Myla—who won't talk to him on the phone, anyway. The script refuses to talk to him as well and he suspects that he'll be the first of at least nine writers on the project.

Having behaved wantonly—and with some other Bambi, not the wife of his friend, never—he has come to rest in this luxurious prison, this fortress of the delicate summer, where in his discreet and lonely evenings at the bar he sits at the table behind the stubby palm tree and writes letters to his children. He remembers Myla at age fifteen in her short shorts, at age thirty in the yellow sundress, at age forty in her garland of freckles, naked, as she waded in the shallows of an Ozark trout stream.

Days turn into weeks. He has never felt so sorry for himself.

Then, wearing a white suit and manufacturing a smile she appears at the door to his bungalow. She's hungry, she says, and tired of eating alone. As he dresses for dinner he fumbles through an incoherent apology, then as they stroll toward the patio, violins playing, she confesses that she recently slept with her psychiatrist. Under his frantic questioning at dinner she reminds him of the doctor's name.

The guy with the beard? The Italian?

I call him *bambino*, she responds.

He covers up his sadness with anger. Totally unethical, he asserts. A woman should be able to trust her psychiatrist.

Copulation, she informs him, was just a form of therapy.

That's all it was, he assures her, for me!

They go through the agony of desserts: chocolate mousse for him and peaches flambé for her.

In the bungalow, later, they bathe themselves in white: the lilies at their bedside table, white silk sheets, her white suit thrown aside, and the white liquids that oil their senses.

9

Beyond the big round bed in Malibu the French doors open onto the beach and surf. In these days his face melts away like wax; he takes blood pressure medicine that cools his desire and watches her freckled skin turn into soft scales.

The children, finished with college, all have loves of their own. Myla and Will stroll the beach recalling the ballgames, boyfriends, and music recitals, and how on occasion each child seemed to speak in a mysterious poetry.

Will's books now fill up a shelf: a novel with glowing reviews, another praised, others not. He reads only biographies and visionary works on astrophysics. Meanwhile, Myla makes lists: groceries, favorite movies, proposed holiday sites, and even a list of her meager jewelry, items she intends to be distributed to children, grandchildren or friends on the occasion of her death. Also a list of things lost: the Murano goblets, a gold locket, one of the twin's guitar, the fancy telescope.

In the circular bed they listen to the echoes of the surf in the room as he rubs ointment into her arthritic hands. When she compliments his touch he asks in his best Bogart tone if she wants to make out, and in their mutual massage, then, they reach for the old fever. The coals beneath the skin are slower to ignite, but afterward he holds her as she sleeps, listening to her breath, and he's overcome by this soft warmth beyond orgasm, this calm, this metamorphosis into permanent afterglow. Then he wonders to himself, okay, will I ever write again and about what, about what?

10

With an assortment of senior cronies they visit the Great Wall, Buddhist temples, the Forbidden City, and China's terra cotta warriors, but what impresses them most is a 90-mile stretch of superhighway, six lanes, built by hand with thousands of workers mixing the cement in wheelbarrows.

In their compartment on the night train to Xian he feels restless and can't sleep, but Myla grows sick and veers into delirium. He presses his palm against her burning forehead and listens as she talks in her sleep. She believes she's on the Blue Train heading toward Cape Town in a movie with Gene Hackman or somewhere in Oklahoma.

The train clings to the side of a mountain as below a dark valley pulls at them. Next morning in the city he devours a cheeseburger for breakfast in the hotel coffee shop and while she continues to sleep he goes for a long walk. On the grounds of a temple with an ancient pagoda he finds a giant prayer bell. Its hammer is a teakwood log suspended on thick chains, and he pays ten yuan to swing it into the echoing bell. For Myla—always clear headed and never ill—he prays the first prayer he has uttered in years.

Back at the hotel, amazingly, her fever has broken and she suggests they might try a little cuddling. When he takes off his clothes and exposes his paunch she smiles and tells him he has the body of a god.

Lord Buddha, she says. That god.

They join themselves like two expensive antiques: good fittings, a few creaking parts, good workmanship.

11

A mountainside in the Ozarks: their last house.

He enjoys lunches with his cronies: three reporters, the doctor, the psychologist, the librarian, and an occasional visitor referred to as the designated listener. Some of them play golf on the weekends, but although most of them arrived in this place because of the fishing none of them actually go for the trout anymore. As a group they favor the written word, sports, and gravy. Their consensus is that good reporting is superior to good or even great fiction. They speak to one another in anecdotes because they know that all ideas are untrue.

One night after supper Will gets a headache, his first in years, and the next morning he can't remember the names of his pals. He doesn't mention this to Myla.

Because their sleep turns restless they sleep in separate bedrooms. In the springtime she goes skiing with their daughter, then comes back to renovate her workshop where she takes up her old hobby, throwing clay pots.

One morning, shaving, Will notices his drooping eye; it looks as though it might slide down his cheek and off his face.

On a moonless midsummer evening Myla and Will sit outdoors in deck chairs gazing off into space: distant stars, the dark winds, and galaxies beyond their vision that they agree they can feel. At death, she muses, their molecules will fly into the cosmos, blown around like so many dandelion particles. Her version of eternity sounds very much like the Grand Tour: visits to faraway constellations, to the great clouds where stars are born, and to a view of how the pieces all fit together. Our personal Unified Field Theory, he says, and he somehow believes all of it. He kisses the bent fingers of his priestess. Molecules don't die, she explains. I've been reading about it, she tells him, and they go on living, behaving quite a lot like little bitty brains with minds of their own.

In late November their sons move Will's bed over by the big window so he can look out on the hills. Father and sons try a few hands of poker, but Will can't keep up, so they listen to music until darkness comes and they can see their faces—so alike, so different—in the window's reflection.

That night Myla comes to his bed and holds him in her arms.

Tell me about the molecules again, he says.

From what we know, she answers, smiling, certain clusters of molecules attract each other. If you split these molecules up, according to scientists, they manage to find each other again. Some scientists—maybe the more religious ones—believe they get back together again in some sort of consciousness. So do I, she says decisively. I believe that, too.

Maybe some of mine and some of yours, he remarks.

After this the lights go out in Galway, along the Amalfi Coast, on Padre Island, at the Safeway store, and in the deepest recesses of molecular memory. The stations of the body fade away: regions of the cortex, the distant toes, and the bloody old heart. He can feel her close and detect that soft, soapy odor, the one that filled the blanket on the grass that night long ago on Lake Dallas. Then the new lights begin to appear, faintly at first: the glow of the North Star, far away Andromeda, and the galaxies beyond all imagination.

Tickets to Nowhere

After he was laid off the oil rig Vernon drove out of Midland, Texas, heading home to Arkansas, but the transmission in his old Ford went out, so he sold the car for junk in Weatherford. He decided to get to the Dallas-Fort Worth airport, buy himself a ticket with his last money, fly home penniless again, and admit that his life was a beer drinking disaster. On the bus to the airport he felt like crying, especially when he passed a string of barbecue joints with their neon beer signs already ablaze.

Late that afternoon he stood in the departure lounge of a commuter airline with a ticket in his hand and forty-six cents in his jeans. He faced a dozen uniformed airline employees behind tall counters. Beyond the counters were assorted gates where small jets were scheduled for such places as Lawton, Harlingen, Wichita Falls, Fayetteville, Muskogee, and Texarkana. He dreaded flying back to Fayetteville, then hitching a ride north to his daddy's farm and another round of family lectures. Vernon was creeping up on forty years of age and looked like grit and sludge: jeans stained with oil, dirty fingernails, thinning hair, and a sweater that had been stuffed down in his tool box too often.

Addled and tired, needing a beer, he stood on one leg then the other, waiting, when he heard an announcement regarding his flight. The plane had been overbooked, so the airline was offering a $200 travel voucher and $20 airport meal ticket to anyone willing to give up his seat and take a later flight.

Vernon hurried to the appropriate counter and addressed a pretty Latin attendant, a girl with a bit of hair on her upper lip.

"That meal voucher," he began, drawling out his words more loudly than he had to. "Is it good for beer or just food?"

Ten minutes later he sat in a bar decorated with Dallas Cowboy photos and football gear. He emptied a schooner of Shiner Bock and nibbled at a shrimp cocktail. Another beer was on order from the bartender who wore a neck brace, a guy who seemed like one of the nicest persons Vernon had ever met. In fact, all the occupants of the bar seemed nice and respectable: upscale folks in suits and dresses, folks with important places to go, bankers and such. In a far corner beneath the overblown photo of a quarterback sat the only unhappy customer, a young woman with her head down, crying, without so much as a glass of water in front of her.

Vernon studied the travel voucher laid out before him.

He wondered if such a prize could be converted into actual cash money and thought, hell, I could damn near buy another used car with this amount. With such speculations, daydreams overtook him. He could drive to Mexico and work with Pemex. Find himself a nice little border cantina. Send a letter to his Baptist daddy with a hundred dollar bill folded inside it, a partial payback.

At the appointed hour he strolled back down the concourse to the commuter gates only to learn that his next flight was now overbooked, too, and that he could receive yet another $200 voucher, two more $20 meal certificates, and a free night's lodging in the swank Airport Sheraton.

Grinning and satisfied with prospects—and with a tiny buzz on—he gathered up his vouchers and certificates and returned to the Cowboy bar to celebrate.

By this time a deep twilight had settled on the airport. The planes beyond the concourse windows looked wildly beautiful, shining with reflected lights. Vernon felt that as if by magic he had been transported into another social class, a cut above the cigarette butts and whanging country music of Midland's honky-tonks and the smelly oil towns of West Texas.

He wished he had a sports jacket.

The Cowboy bar was packed with a new crowd except for that sad girl who occupied the corner table. Her face was now turned to the wall, though she didn't seem to be crying. Swathed in black and wearing a ratty black turban—sort of Oriental gothic—she looked hungry, thirsty, stood up, and stranded.

He strolled over and offered her his extra $20 meal ticket.

"It's good for booze, too," he assured her.

"Do I look like I need charity?"

"No, not a'tall, but what'll you have?" he persisted. "I got money for drinks and dinner on these vouchers and, well, tell you the truth, I'm celebrating. My luck turned good."

"Then I'll have a glass of red vermouth with ice," she said, and her voice was formal and uppity, sort of British, yet not.

Vernon had two more beers with her and they split a bag of potato chips. She said her name was Marbella and, yes, she was stranded, stuck in the airport for almost two days with a worthless credit card that her poet boyfriend had maxed out.

"So he's, what, a professional poet?" Vernon asked, looking into the mascara smear of her eyes.

"Nobody's a professional poet," Marbella informed him, waving a potato chip. "I mean, Wallace Stevens worked at an insurance company and T.S. Eliot was an editor at Faber and Faber. Poets have other jobs. And they're sometimes fakes and neurotics, but at their best they create images tossed up against the crush of destiny."

"That's for sure," Vernon replied, trying to be agreeable.

"For years I tried to cultivate the literary language myself," she admitted. "But now I'm older and considerably more hip and I want to get rid of it. If I ever finish my dissertation, I probably won't even teach. Because I'll crave a greater reality. I mean, a doctorate can just mire one down in the second hand life. But one wants a reality that truly confirms itself. What's that on your jeans?"

"Right here? Grease."

"Exactly what I'm talking about. Hard reality. You're wearing it. Zero at the bone. The dirt of the real world. Did you say you have another meal voucher? Suddenly, I'm starving. And if I'm going to sleep in those god awful airport chairs tonight I need to eat."

"You don't have to sleep here in the airport," Vernon told her. "You can share a room with me at the hotel. I've got a room voucher, too."

"No sex," she said, agreeing.

"Whatever," he answered, and for a moment they gave each other a look of worldly insouciance—her look considerably more successful than his—then they went off to the Big Tex Buffet Corral.

After a full meal they rode the tram to the hotel.

As they presented themselves at the registration desk, Marbella stood aside while Vernon signed in, and he was grateful because she looked a bit like a vampire, or, at best, the soloist in a rock group. On request, he showed the desk clerk his Arkansas driver's license with a photo that made him look like a convict, and the clerk sniffed at it, stamped the room voucher, and pushed a plastic key card across the marble desktop.

The room was far better than anything Vernon had ever occupied: plush golden carpets, overstuffed chairs, a 35-inch TV set, a king-sized bed, and a tiled bath with a single white terrycloth robe that Marbella quickly confiscated.

Later, draped in that robe and sitting cross-legged in the middle of the bed, drying her hair, she watched Vernon pacing the room and talking about his new idea. Her shiny brown hair looked much better than that ratty turban, and her knees, tanned and pretty, poked out of the robe.

"I know this airline and it overbooks every day and passes out them vouchers," he said, pacing. "Two years ago when I was pretty flush and headin' home for Thanksgiving they was doin' it. Anyhow, if we could figure out how to turn the vouchers into cash money we could make ourselves a fine livin' right here in the goddamned terminal. It'd be indoor work and air-conditioned. I know it'd be a hell of a lot better'n being a roustabout."

"Go on," Marbella encouraged him.

"See, we study the flights that are constantly overbooked. We sign up, never go anyplace, and collect vouchers. All we gotta do is get bumped off flights. We eat on food vouchers. They got places in this airport complex that don't even serve barbecue. Also, we figure the late flights and stay in these fancy hotels."

"You're including me in this?

"Why, sure, between us we can make plenty if we unload them vouchers."

Inside those dark pools of mascara Marbella's eyes were wide and alert with possibilities. Meanwhile, Vernon, having no idea of the full effect of his money making scheme, paced the room, stopped at the little mini-bar, removed another Shiner beer, and popped another cap. He touched the cold bottle to his temple so that he could think more clearly and continued to pace.

"Somebody will buy them damned vouchers," he went on. "I've seen newspaper ads. In the classified. Outfits that pay for airline vouchers and certificates."

"By god, you're an entrepreneur," Marbella said with a sigh.

"We could get rich. Take ourselves a real little holiday now and then. I'd like to see the Caribbean, wouldn't you?"

"You're a tycoon all right," she told him. "Come over here."

Vernon sat down on the bedside, taking a quick glance into the open robe. A stray thought hit him: he had assumed that the middle of this king-sized bed would be banked up with a wall of pillows but maybe it wouldn't. As he considered this, Marbella walked across the bed on her knees and began massaging his neck and shoulders.

"My dissertation is on forms of deconstruction, but not exactly," she began, working on his tight muscles. "It's more like the relationship between catastrophe theory and creativity. Not that I'm all that personally confident about psychoanalysis and literature. Far from it, God, Vernon just relax. Anyway, my therapist warned me that I could become obsessed with this idea, but, see, psychic energy can actually become a systematic. So what exactly do you like to read?"

"The sports pages," Vernon sighed, giving in to her touch.

"Naturally. Game theory, sure, I should've known. Actually, that might be helpful in defining the catastrophe of creative origins. Let's see, help me, I'm looking for the right metaphor here, but what I want to say, actually, is how destruction is a primitive form of possession."

"Like offense and defense," Vernon offered, thinking of football.

"Exactly! That's wonderful, yes! Oh, God, Vernon, you have such a deep basic instinct for life! Here, kiss me."

Their kiss, long and wet, resulted in the robe falling away, their bodies entwined, and her breathless confession.

"Vernon, Sweet, my name's not really Marbella," she told him as they ended the kiss. "It's actually Bobbie Rae Smith."

"Well, sure, okay," he managed, nuzzling close.

"Marbella is a Spanish island," she informed him.

"Hell," he replied, "don't worry about it."

By evening of the following day they had collected six travel vouchers, an equal number of meal certificates, and hotel accommodations for two. No longer encased in her conspicuous mascara, turban, and gothic black, Bobbie Rae wore her current disguise: reading glasses, a beret, and a long Picasso scarf. Although

Vernon felt euphoric and slightly tipsy from all his beer breaks, he still worried about how to convert their treasures into cash.

As they sat in the Wrangler Bar pondering this, each of them preoccupied with just how much in love the other might be, a large black man slid into a chair at their table. They assumed he was just another traveler in the crowded room, so lowered their voices and continued their business.

"I wish we could keep a hotel room all day, so I could change into my different clothes," Bobbie Rae complained. "Coin lockers and the ladies room are a hassle."

"We got a few kinks in our workday," Vernon agreed.

"How true," added the black man, leaning back and grinning. "Like that wad of vouchers stuffed down in her handbag."

"I beg your pardon," said Bobbie Rae in her most arch and formal accent.

"I've enjoyed watchin' you two," the black man went on, grinning.

In the breathless pause that followed he opened his wallet and showed them a shiny badge: Airport Security. Both Bobbie Rae and Vernon now raised their eyes to the blue name tag pinned on the man's lapel, a tag that bore a single name: McCreedy. From that they lifted their gaze toward his seemingly malevolent smile.

"Now just lookee here," Vernon told him, braving it out. "We just like to travel places. No harm in that. Or in collectin' ourselves some vouchers."

"If you plan to travel," McCreedy answered, grinning, "you might decide which direction you aim to go. So far today you've bought tickets to Muskogee, Brownsville, Memphis, and El Paso. As I see it, that's north, south, east, and west."

"We're saving up for a trip to Budapest," Bobbie Rae put in, her voice achieving a truly regal accent.

"Now don't get smart. You haven't done anything illegal and I don't aim to arrest you."

"Then it's no business of yours," Vernon added, sensing a small advantage.

"No, at the moment it ain't. But if you intend to unload them vouchers I can always offer my humble services."

"We don't need no partner," Vernon said, although he was now sure that they already had one.

"You can peddle the vouchers to a couple of agencies here in Dallas, but they'll take fifty percent or more of face value,"

McCreedy confided. "I can get us a much better deal. My take will be fifty bucks per voucher and a daily meal certificate."

"You are a crooked cop," Bobbie Rae said slowly, failing to keep the admiration out of her voice.

"Trust no other kind," McCreedy replied.

As it turned out, McCreedy had three kids, a wife with a bad back, and a night job standing guard over nine acres of discarded automobile tires. He explained that he had to get rid of that extra night work.

"My nerves are all frayed and I'm listless all day here at the airport," he said, leveling with them. "I'm crazy with too much coffee and my sleep patterns are shot. Also, it's humiliating protecting a goddamned mound of worn out tires that nobody would ever steal."

"You poor thing," Bobbie Rae told him, and Vernon couldn't tell if a little sarcasm leaked into her tone or not.

Over a second round of coffee, beer, and red vermouth they struck a deal on the vouchers.

The scheme had flaws—a few times they didn't get bumped as expected, so ended up with paid tickets—but they kept at it for ten days. McCreedy's wife donated clothes, so that Bobbie Rae could keep up her disguises and Vernon became attached to a cubbyhole bar called Sagebrush Junction that served frozen pints of his favorite Shiner Bock.

They worked steady and made fair money, although Bobbie Rae had a few criticisms. "You trying to get a master's degree in beer drinking?" she asked. When she turned sassy like that, Vernon actually adored her. Sometimes she went off into the concept zone, talking absolute nonsense, but her angelic and wildly serious expressions on such occasions also won his heart. Although the deceits and gambles of the day were exciting, he now lived for the nights. He found himself crash landing into love: a real flame out, a tailspin.

After a few more hard days in the commuter lounge, though, Bobbie Rae became even more petulant. One night she even criticized his lovemaking techniques.

"Vernon, it is the end of the twentieth century, you know, and the female clit—like all major continents—has been discovered."

"Yes'm," he said, and went about his duties.

In calmer moments he decided that Bobbie Rae's attitude, after all, was just what he needed. He could count on her, he figured, to take care of checkbooks, bills, and business matters that he didn't have a knack for. Like having a pet bulldog: a confrontive soul mate who'd face down the phone company, the tax man, and maybe even his hard-nosed daddy.

One night, sprawled out beside her in the fever of afterglow, he said, "Bobbie Rae, I want you to meet my family up in Arkansas."

"No way," she answered sleepily. "I'm not good with families."

Afterward, he gazed at the ceiling wondering why he'd said such a goofy thing. Did he want to marry her? Was he over-committed? Or did he just want to turn Bobbie Rae loose on his daddy? With that last thought he grinned, closed his eyes, and soon fell asleep.

The next morning, McCreedy paid them several hundred dollars, but issued a warning.

"Somebody might be onto us," he told them. "Might be good if you two knocked off for a few days."

"C'mon, we need to keep at it," Vernon complained. "What makes you suspicious?"

"This guy at the airline says they might stop giving out vouchers because they're worried about abuse. He didn't mention anybody in particular, but I'm frettin' over why he said this to me."

Vernon suggested to Bobbie Rae that they might fly down to Laredo and cross over into Mexico for a couple of days, but she just sniffed at the idea. "We just saw our first money," she argued. "We don't need some shoddy low-rent holiday." Her voice did that thing again: shoddy sounded as if it had been dropped by a duchess.

For another day, then, they tried to figure out the overbooked flights, succeeded in getting bumped, and collected. During the lulls Vernon sat on a stool at Sagebrush Junction talking to a salesman about an old idea of his: Popsicles flavored with gin, beer, bourbon, or rum. It was his favorite beer joint topic of conversation and he was explaining his marketing ideas when he happened to glance out at the concourse to see Bobbie Rae talking to a long-haired guy who had an acoustic guitar strapped to his backside. Somehow Vernon immediately knew: the poet was back.

Vernon took a deep breath, gathered himself, and casually strolled out to introduce himself. When he extended his hand the guy just kept talking to Bobbie Rae, ignoring him, and he was a snotty type, clearly, who had taught Bobbie Rae all her phony accents.

Vernon persisted, interrupting once more.

"Yeah, just a minute," the poet told him, and continued his long explanation and apology, asserting that he had looked everywhere for Bobbie Rae and that the credit card was actually good, so that it annoyed Vernon that she would stand there listening to all this.

"You know that's a by god lie," Vernon told the poet, hoping that the guy might throw a punch.

"Marbella, just go over to that newsstand," said the poet. "Go over there and charge something on the card. You'll see that I'm telling the truth."

"He's bluffin'," Vernon persisted.

"Do you mind?" the poet asked in a voice that sounded faintly French.

"Vernon, please, just let us alone for a minute," she asked.

Disgusted with both of them and mad at himself for caring, Vernon turned and stalked back to the bar, where the drunken salesman seemed eager to discuss Popsicles flavored with booze. Vernon's hands shook with anger and he hated his drawl: a hick voice, a voice with a twang like everyone else's on the rigs. With elocution lessons, he felt, he could've been district supervisor of something.

In their hotel scarcely an hour later Vernon saw all the bad signs: Bobbie Rae had returned to gothic black, wouldn't talk about the poet, and wouldn't go out to dinner.

"C'mon, Bobbie Rae, I was thinkin' about that fancy restaurant over at the Marriott. White tablecloths and wine. How about it?"

"Will you please call me Marbella?" she replied, not looking at him. "I've been trying to get away from Bobbie Rae all my life."

"Okay, then, Marbella, are you going back to that poet or what?"

"I don't know."

"Well, see, I'm pretty much in love with you, whatever your name is. And there, I've said it out loud."

"Pretty much? Is that quite a lot by your definition?"

"It's a whole hell of a lot for any roustabout and for me especially," he said, and he broke into laughter at his own clever down-home wit.

"Then that forces me to tell you, Vernon, that roustabouts are the sort of men I've been avoiding all of my life, too! Also, bricklayers, dry wallers, mechanics, city workers, truck drivers, and janitors!"

He hated that they argued, but came back with, "See here, then, musicians are the worst of the worst! And that ain't no fancy poet! He's just another deadbeat guitar pickin' asshole sonavabitch as anyone can plainly see!"

"He's a fine folk singer," she put in defensively, and seemed on the verge of tears.

"Besides, a roustabout saved your pretty butt just a short time ago! Or don't you recall that you was sleepin' out on the concourse with not a single meal certificate to your name?"

By this time she was packing. Disappointment overwhelmed him, yet he blamed himself; once again his confession of love arrived as the object of his affection banged out the door. And he felt the finality of it like a sudden and unexpected slap. Say nothing, he warned himself; stay cool and keep your self-respect.

Yet he asked, "You got someplace to go?"

"I'll manage."

"Then that means you won't be there at the commuter airline counters tomorrow?"

"You bet I won't," she said sharply.

He watched her toss clothing into her bag, including some of McCreedy's wife's things. He wanted to bite down on his lip and keep his silence, but it all hurt too much.

"No kiss, then, and no fare thee wells?"

"Vernon, I just don't feel like any of that."

"Bein' mad at me is something you've had to invent," he said evenly, as if he were analyzing the catastrophe from a great distance. "Because I ain't done nothin' wrong, Bobbie Rae, and you can't say otherwise. You've just worked up this mad so's you can leave."

She was crying now, but scooping her heavy bag and struggling to the door.

"I'll look for you in the airport in case you get stuck here again," he called after her, but his pathetic words of bitter good will were spoken to the closed door.

He sat down in an armchair to get his breath. The room reeled and he felt its black dizziness, so sat, addled, his wires torn loose and his confusion so complete that he didn't even want a beer. He sat there until twilight turned into night, then he staggered the few steps to the bed, crawled in, and covered up.

After a night of restless sleep he got up and went in search of McCreedy, but didn't find him. He phoned the McCreedy house, got no answer, so at noon took the flight to Laredo. By evening, he figured, he'd be across the border drinking Carta Blanca with a wedge of lemon stuck in the bottleneck.

On the plane, lost in his thoughts, his losses seemed to go back years and years: lousy grades in school, his daddy's constant bad humor, lost jobs, temporary women, places that briefly held promise then just as quickly passed away. He sat looking down at the clouds trying to reconcile it all: a busted transmission here, a pretentious woman with two names there, schemes and beer dreams, too many long drives on sad highways, games never won, tickets to nowhere. Losses, losses, and more losses: days would arrive, he knew, when he couldn't shoulder a length of pipe anymore or carry a coil of heavy chain up the platform ladder of a rig. After that, what? Real infirmity and old age because a working-man's body breaks down as the injuries pile up. Terrible losses. He'd die up in Arkansas, he figured, in his old boyhood room with his toy soldiers in the same cigar box underneath the creaking bed.

Why, for that matter, was he going to Laredo? A guy chases his losses like a bad woman, pursuing them without shame, he guessed, kissing the dirt of the world, trying for more humiliation.

A man who sat next to him on the plane, a man who smelled of expensive after-shave and peppermint, turned to him after they had been in flight for half an hour, smiled, and asked if he was headed to Mexico for a holiday. The man's gentle decency and courtesy made him want to cry.

"Well, no sir, I'm goin' down to work for Pemex if I can get on," Vernon told him. "To put it straight, I reckon I'm going to compete with all the poor Mexicans for one of their jobs, but oilfield work is all I know."

"Good luck," the man said, looking back at his magazine.

"'Course, I got some ideas, too," Vernon went on. "Business concepts and such. You know Popsicles, don't you?"

Looking for Greywolf

Skyler finally agreed to attend one of the family reunions down in Austin, but only because she heard that Perry, her wildly attractive cousin, was supposed to be present after an absence of more than a dozen years. Skyler had been on all the continents, of course, while the rest of the family had been to the Cotton Bowl. She read Umberto Eco and they read Jackie Collins. She understood the real Karen Blixen—the one who slept with young boys while suffering from syphilis, who drank too much, and who often ran at overstuffed chairs head first—while the rest of the family had enjoyed the movie with Robert Redford, she supposed, and especially the soundtrack.

But Cousin Perry, well: he was a story she couldn't resist. So she found Doctor Teddy's house up in the hills—a big sprawl in a neighborhood of similar villas—and stepped into the blast of Texas heat: the temperature around one hundred, a gulf breeze drenching the afternoon with a gagging humidity, lawn sprinklers clacking away.

She entered a side door off the driveway where she was confronted by a pretty teenager whose mouth dropped open and who greeted her, helplessly, by asking, "God, who are you?"

Skyler supposed, okay, maybe I'm a bit overdressed, maybe I'm wearing a tad too much black for midsummer, but she answered without skipping a beat. "I'm the legendary bitch," she replied. "Skyler the snob. The slut. The one who went away."

The girl nodded in awed recognition.

Skyler swept toward the laughter in the kitchen where she heard Julia's loud drawl. Julia, Uncle Teddy's your second wife, was doing one of her riffs—this time on her old man's droopy scrotum—but as Skyler appeared the two of them went into a noisy hello, kissing the air beside each other's cheeks, hugging, and trading insults.

"Goddamn, trust you to wear black," Julia yelled out. "And look at them rhinestones!"

Julia knew both diamonds and grammar, of course, but she was the family's stand-up comic and sometimes employed a clever cruelty, like Skyler herself, to score a few painful bull's eyes on a slower-witted family member.

"I wore black 'cause y'all keep dying faster than I can keep up," Skyler answered. "And look at you! You're downright skinny except for that little pooch."

"That's my wine cellar," said Julia, patting her tummy, and they began a long vulgar litany about bad skin, plastic surgeons, getting old, pooches, and tucks until Julia went back to the subject of old Doctor Teddy's scrotum once again.

"He's got all this leftover skin down there," she hooted. "I think he could cover a small car with it! Like a little MG. You know, like the covers they drape over 'em at night?"

Laughter went up again from Julia's audience of three wives. A timid woman with bad teeth—her hand covering her mouth—enjoyed the riff clearly more than she meant to.

"Honey, you are far too pretty," Skyler told the teenager who had let her into the house. "You gotta be illegitimate."

"Paula is Buddy Ray's daughter," Julia said. "By which wife we're not exactly sure."

"Celia," said Paula, naming her mother with a tiny grin.

"Well, Honey, you're a looker and you don't have to hang around family reunions—or hasn't anyone told you that?"

By this time Skyler had accepted a beer and was moving outside to the deck overlooking the pool. Julia followed. Across the way sat another cluster of overweight females who waved, then quickly turned to one another by way of identifying the new arrival. Baby back ribs and chicken wings adorned the platters on the poolside tables. Noisy children bobbed and splashed underneath the diving board and from the shade of a plastic canopy Doctor Teddy and the elderly males lifted their cigars in greeting.

"Ah, there he is," Skyler said, looking toward the thick-shouldered man who dangled his feet off the side of the pool.

"Yep, that's Perry," Julia confirmed. "Still a hunk."

"My lord, I'd tell him yes even if his question wasn't exactly clear," Skyler said with a sigh.

"In the normal definitions of incest," Julia asked with a low growl of laughter, "do cousins count?"

His hair was streaked with gray now and tied in a ponytail, but Perry had the same muscular body, deeply tanned, that used to excite Skyler and the other girls when they went swimming at Barton Springs in the old days. As they stood on the deck admiring him she told Julia about seeing him once, years ago, sitting in a convertible outside her mother's house on Blue Water Drive, sitting in the open car with his arm around a feverish young woman who nuzzled his neck and kissed him.

"I must've been, oh, eleven years old," Skyler recalled. "And I assumed, well, that everything was hot but innocent, so I just strolled over to the car. You know, just for mischief. They were both buck-naked and she was sitting, well, in the receptive mode, but in spite of it Perry looked up, smiled sweetly, said hi, and managed to begin a very courteous and casual conversation with me. The girl was uneasy, but I understood that he didn't want to embarrass me or hurt my feelings because of my blunder. Anyway, we talked for a while. I tried to look into his eyes—or at the sky—then finally I made my escape."

"Damn," Julia said, grinning, and they leaned together, trying to avoid gazing across the pool in his direction.

The afternoon soon turned into food, drink, and all the white lies about jobs and children. Skyler made her way around the pool, moving from one cluster of forced smiles to the next. Everyone asked about her husband, Kip, and made her explain again and again his specialty in the stock market: the buying and selling of first issues. One aunt said, well, at least he wears a nice suit and tie to the office, but Skyler said, no, actually jeans, and Doctor Teddy, who rubbed his fingers through his mop of white hair when he pontificated, allowed that many business executives these days, including Bill Gates, often dressed down—at least on Fridays.

"So where is Kip, anyhow?" Doctor Teddy asked.

"He really wanted to come with me," Skyler lied, studying the old man. The doctor owned ranch land rather than stocks and had outlived all his hard drinking younger brothers including Skyler's father, whose highest achievement had been as manager of a bowling alley. Doctor Teddy's only remaining pride was poor

Julia, who made fun of him, spent his money, and nowadays refused to sleep in the same room with him. The old man had a pious tilt of the chin and would have claimed all the bragging rights in the family except that his only son, Perry, the object of Skyler's sidelong glances all afternoon, had gone into an infamous tailspin of pot and peyote, wasting his life and ruining Doctor Teddy's perfect score.

"I admire your husband," Doctor Teddy intoned, smoothing a tuft of snowy hair beside his ear.

"He sends his best," Skyler managed.

"He's successful. Very. And a clever fellow. I enjoy talking business with him. A shame you two could never have children."

"Some folks think sex is a lot of fun and children are the punishment," Skyler offered with a little laugh. But the flippancy didn't work at all and the doctor stiffened. Only Julia, standing nearby and overhearing the remark, snorted with laughter and turned away.

The doctor stared into his glass of bourbon, frowning, and Skyler promised herself that she wouldn't ever again try sarcasm, irony, or a verbal counterpunch with the old coot.

Later, Perry sat on the diving board toying with a plate of food, so Skyler picked up a brownie, strolled over, and sat close beside him so their shoulder touched.

"You handsome damn brute," she began.

"Hey, good lookin'," he responded, and he was much the same: wildly masculine with an easy smile, yet with a strange and distracting intensity.

"I was thinking about you and your convertible."

"My old Ford? Really?"

"I was eleven years old when I saw you sitting in it with your girlfriend, remember?"

She gave his shoulder a deliberate bump with hers.

"I sorta hoped you'd forgotten that."

"Never. But tell me, how are you, Perry?"

"Bummed out."

"You look as though you'd rather be someplace else. So why're you here?"

"I touch base every four of five years, but I never see you. So what provoked you to come?"

"Maybe I had a notion to see you," she said, flirting.

"You're still married and living in Memphis, aren't you?"

"See, you know all about me," she said, smiling, and she bent forward and turned so she could catch his line of vision because he wouldn't quite look at her. "But I've lost track of you, so I came to catch up. Tell me what's going on."

She already knew most of it. After Perry finished his course work for a doctoral degree in philosophy, he ran off with a professor's wife. His dissertation remained forever unwritten and the wife had family money that kept him in style for a couple of years. He ended up in the mountains of New Mexico doing peyote with some cult. At that point the family in Austin didn't hear from him for ten years.

"You know I have an Indian name, don't you?" he asked.

"An Indian name? Really? What?"

"Greywolf. That's who I am now."

"You turned into an Indian?" Skyler asked, trying to keep the sarcasm out of her voice.

He shrugged and grinned at her. "Loony, isn't it?"

"Yeah, it sure as hell is," she agreed. "But is that a code name? You're not a full time drug dealer with a code name, are you?"

"No, not at all."

They sat in silence while she waited for him to elaborate, but he kept to himself while she finished her brownie.

"How old are you?" he finally asked.

"Almost forty," she lied, trimming off a couple of years. When he asked he still didn't look at her, yet his voice fell into an intimate tone.

"Well, we haven't much time left, you and I," he said, and she didn't know exactly what he meant. Was it an offhand remark about how old they were becoming or was it more personal, about the two of them and maybe some mutual destiny? She wanted to ask for clarification, but at that moment he leaned into her, shoulder to shoulder, and she felt a curious shudder go through her body.

"You know, Austin's a mess nowadays," he began, going into an environmental ramble Skyler only half listened to. "These hills can't support all the houses being built. I used to roam around those cliffs out there hunting rabbits, but now everything's paved. We're paving the whole continent, Skyler, we really are, and most Americans are like bacteria covering the landscape."

Something was happening while he talked. Her fingers trembled and she knew she couldn't possibly stand on her feet. Trapped in his force field, giddy, she worried that she might faint.

He continued to talk. New Mexico. The wind in the trees. Free as a hawk. Etcetera.

"When the snows start in the mountains I go down to a place in Mexico on the Sea of Cortez," he went on. She heard only the sound of his voice, a voice like echoes over water, and her body quivered and melted away, and her emotions were somewhat erotic, a tremor down inside some forgotten zone, sexual, yet not.

As if she had been in a trance she woke up to find Perry standing on the far side of the pool drinking club soda and talking with that pretty niece and with a fat man whose cheeks were webbed with dark veins. Skyler sat on the diving board, addled, until at last Julia arrived, sat beside her, touched her, and whispered, "Damn, Honey, you okay?"

"We've got to talk," Skyler managed.

By ten o'clock that evening all the relatives had gone to their motels or into one wing or another of Doctor Teddy's spacious house, so Skyler and Julia sagged into an overstuffed sofa, drank straight coffee, and went on about Perry.

"They gave him that name," Julia revealed. "Greywolf. He's some kind of tribal medicine man."

"Like a guru? C'mon, Perry's a Baptist."

"Used to be. And I know, it's real spooky. Last year before Uncle Bates died he went looking for Perry. Out to New Mexico in the mountains. It took him a week to find him. I think he wanted to ask Greywolf some kind of religious question. Did I tell you this?"

"No, go on."

"It just got into Uncle Bates' mind to do this thing. Anyway, when he came back he wouldn't say much. We all figured he'd been told something special and we asked him about it, but he just kept quiet about it, then he died."

Skyler hid behind her coffee cup, watching Julia over the rim. She liked Julia, but wondered if Doctor Teddy's second wife might have a mystical side. Julia, of course, had always seemed practical to a fault, a woman waiting for the old codger to kick off so she could gather up the loot, but something earnest in Julia's voice made her speculate. Uncle Bates had gone on this pilgrimage, heard some truth or another, then passed on, and Julia seemed to believe that something authentic had transpired.

"Well, where's our big ole Greywolf now?" Skyler inquired.

"In a bedroom down the hallway," Julia revealed.

"Which wing?"

"The pool wing. Second door on the left. You have a notion to commune with the great spirit?"

"There are varieties of religious experience," Skyler said with a sigh, assuming that Julia would pick up the allusion. "When I was fifteen I went to church camp. That's where I first got laid. Two weeks of hiking, swimming, vespers, and the head lifeguard. I mean, theological transcendence. Ecstasy."

They decided they needed stronger drink.

After two glasses of Irish whiskey at the kitchen counter Julia gracefully went off to bed in her private suite far from Doctor Teddy's snoring. Skyler returned to the den, finished off her drink, sat around, sucked on the ice cubes, and finally went in search of her cousin.

His covers were mussed, but he wasn't there, so she roamed the hallways, then went through empty bathrooms, a little TV alcove, and the whole east wing before she circled outside to the deck and pool. She found him asleep in one of the big inflated inner tubes, his beautiful legs draped over the side. She watched him for a while, trying to gather her thoughts, but they would not be assembled, so she took off her clothes and tried to get inside the tube with him, making the rubber squeak as she slid down on top of him. All this finally got his attention.

"Skyler?" he asked sleepily, lifting his hands from her.

"It's okay. You can touch me," she whispered.

As his fingers settled on her bare skin, he confessed, "Sorry, I'm stoned. Very sorry."

"We can take our time," she assured him.

Their limbs squeaked around into awkward angles.

At that moment a large naked man appeared on the other side of the pool and without saying anything, trying to avoid detection, Skyler and Perry attempted to sink out of sight in their rubber tube. It was the man with purple veins in his cheeks and as he poked out his belly and began urinating into the pool he resembled a contented, fat, sleepy Buddha there beneath the summer stars. At that point Skyler recognized him: Cousin

Tilden, with about forty additional pounds around his middle since last seen.

Perry's face was now pressed against her as their breathing mingled. For a moment she decided that all her expectations would soon be satisfied and tried to devise a strategy for mounting him in the impossible confines of the inner tube. I could go there, she found herself thinking, if he could just go there. She loved the feel of their nakedness and if Cousin Tilden could just finish his business—he seemed to flow on like the River Ganges—she calculated that she could make a successful twist.

Then, once again, she began that violent trembling.

Something from his body seemed to move through her like a current and her shaking became an electric pulse. "Oh god," she managed, and his arms closed around her, sheltering her inside that stupid rubberized womb as her hands and fingers became alive apart from her, twitching, and her torso jerked, thrusting upward in a spasm that resembled a sexual movement, yet wasn't. She began to cry uncontrollably. Meanwhile fat Cousin Tilden went on pissing, his head thrown back as he gawked at the sky, his mouth open and his belly pooched out as he remained oblivious to any activity in the rubber tube across the way.

As Skyler wept, her body betraying her, convulsing, Perry, in a hoarse whisper said, "There, there now," and tried to console her until she felt a wilting embarrassment. She wanted to run, but her trembling legs wouldn't let her. Why am I here? What am I doing back in Texas? I adore my husband and I'm in a rubber tube with my cousin who's some idiot medicine man. And why am I crying and shaking and why won't it stop?

At Kip's office his western windows overlooked the churning brown waters of the Mississippi as it flowed through Memphis. The north view took in The Pyramid, its crystal angles reflecting the sky. Skyler had decorated the office interior herself: a masculine cherry wood, red brick and leather, a blue tiled kitchen, a massive white bath with gold fixtures, and a single bedroom done up in the colors of deep autumn. Occasionally she slept with Kip at the workplace—the top floor of an old riverside warehouse—after they had been to dinner at Raji, Paulette's or the Peabody when they were slightly tipsy.

Kip excited her, though the excitement sometimes seemed to reach a danger zone. He was a gambler and a winner, often buying millions of dollars of a new offering in a morning, then hoping its price climbed in the afternoon. He often drove down to the Tunica casinos on weekends or flew to Cabo or Dallas for poker games with his buddies. He tried rock climbing, sky diving, and tried to deal with all the women and girls. Kip wasn't particularly handsome, but had the direct gaze of an intelligent buccaneer and the gambler's reckless aura, so even if Skyler draped herself around him the girls still came on to him. They forced him to say no until sometimes he didn't, but his cheating worked on Skyler like a strange intoxicant, a crazy elixir. His longest fling was with a former beauty queen, a busty woman who lasted just six weeks and who thought Machu Picchu, he later told Skyler, was possibly an Italian wine. Skyler's vengeance for those miserable six weeks was a brief fling of her own: a visiting British symphony conductor who had gobs of culture, she confided in Kip, and a great accent, but few erections and no money at all. They howled with laughter over their stupidities, reconciled, and went on a cruise to the Greek isles. They had rowdy sex and promised never again. He bought her more Limoges and a three-carat sapphire. She decorated his office bedroom in a new color, sage, and they exhausted themselves in another round of sexual acrobatics and, once more, their healing laughter.

They considered themselves flamboyant and impervious—and deeply in love—and when she came back from the reunion in Austin she talked on and on about Julia, but couldn't bring herself to mention Perry. Doubt crept in: did she still hold a grudge about that beauty queen? Why'd she throw herself at her cousin like that? And what about all that nervous trembling? Didn't she adore Kip? Julia, she said, talking on and on about her vulgar and hilarious cousin, was going to write e-mails to her and they were absolutely going to be friends for a long time to come.

On the Friday after her return Kip made reservations at Chez Phillippe and she had visions of a nice meal, a stroll back up the street to the office, a second bottle of wine, and some hello sex in the sage room. She wore a new black sheath and the knockout sapphire. And, okay, nothing actually happened with Perry, so I'll probably tell Kip about my cousin the medicine man, she decided. I'll keep it impersonal and comic because as everything turned out, well, that was how it was.

At dinner, famished, she ordered the caramelized salmon, but when the waiter departed she looked up to find Kip unusually somber.

"Anything wrong?" she asked, smiling and without the least premonition.

"I might as well get to it," he said. "There's somebody else. It's serious."

"Now, damnit, Kip, did you bring me out in public to tell me a thing like that?" In spite of herself her voice rose and her Texas drawl crept in.

"Sorry. I figure I'll be sleeping at the office by myself after tonight."

She stared at him, but he lowered his gaze.

"All right. Who is it?"

"Well, you don't exactly know her."

"Not exactly? What's that mean?"

"Okay, you know Elise Donovan?"

"Elise? We're on the goddamned symphony guild together! What in hell do you see in Elise?"

"It's not Elise. It's her daughter, Chrissie."

"Chrissie Donovan? Goddamn, Kip, she's thirteen years old!"

"She's twenty," Kip corrected her. "And Skyler, please, keep your voice down."

"Chrissie's twenty? Jesus, Kip!"

"Don't yell," he pleaded. "We need to talk this out."

"You're more than twice her age and you'll be tired of her in a month! I wish you hadn't even told me about her!"

"I had to. She's pregnant."

"Fucking Jesus," Skyler shouted at him. "That can be fixed! Give me a goddamned coat hanger!"

They sat in silence. If he urged her one more time to stay calm, she'd break something over his head. He reached out for her hand, but she withdrew it as realization arrived.

"You actually want this baby," she managed, and the words gagged her.

"I don't know why, but, yes, I do."

"Oh, Kip, we promised each other," she said, and now her voice became a forlorn whisper. "We said we didn't want children, remember? Just each other. That was our deal. I stayed thin for you and gave up my child bearing years because you said that's what you wanted."

"Things change," he said to the silverware, unable to look at her. She knew they'd never laugh at this and the knowledge became a terrible hemorrhage deep down.

"Kip, even before we married we agreed. I can't start over and have a baby with somebody else. That part of me's used up. Oh, god, this is the worst thing that could possibly happen."

"Not at all," he argued, concentrating on the tines of his fork. "You'll have plenty of money, Skyler, and you're one of the great looking women, better than ever, really, and cultured, and at the top of your game, and—"

"What's my game?" she interrupted. "It's you, Kip, and always has been! Say this isn't happening. Tell me you'll have Chrissie's little womb all flushed out, then we'll go on a cruise somewhere."

"I want a son," he said coldly, and she knew the whole affair was well along, that Chrissie Donovan must be months pregnant, and that they already had an ultrasound to determine the baby's sex. Knowing this, suddenly, she began to backtrack: Kip sent her off to Austin with this thing in full swing. Weeks and weeks of deceit had gone by before that. Did something in me know, she asked herself, and is that why I turned to Cousin Perry?

A waiter stood at her elbow bearing a dish of salmon, a bright smile on his face.

"Get the hell away from us," she told him, and he retreated with only a glance at Kip, who wouldn't look up.

She tried to recall the last month, but got a blur. Let's see, she prompted herself, when did we go down to New Orleans for that party and why did he come back early?

Kip, meanwhile, was mumbling about the value of the house, back accounts, and settlements that would require lawyers. In the midst of these hideous practicalities she rose from the table and aimed herself at the door. Her eyes filled with tears, so she miscalculated, bumped a table with her hip, and knocked over a glass of red wine beside a man's overcooked steak. Then she staggered, grabbing a woman's shoulder to steady herself, and felt that hemorrhage spewing up into her throat as she made her way out of the restaurant.

In less than a month Kip and Chrissie lived together in a bright new house out in Grove Park, another suburban mansion replete with nursery and lifestyle. When Kip phoned, once, about business, he mentioned that he had taken up golf.

He had domesticated himself.

Skyler spent the rest of the summer in crying jags, two brutal inebriations, phone calls to Memphis acquaintances who didn't care, sleepless nights, and a weight loss that gave her, she decided, not a gaunt new beauty but a faded blight.

She thought of phoning Julia, but didn't want the Texas family to celebrate her pain.

Lawyers converged and Kip turned out to be generous: the house, the Limoges, paintings, a cash settlement and alimony. All the objects seemed to turn against her and memories became knives. She considered finding a disreputable river captain, some old man with tobacco spittle at the corners of his mouth and a willingness to be paid for his mischief. It occurred to her to fill up the Jaguar—her beloved car—with all the items that so offended her now: the Miro, the teakwood Buddha, the Wedgewood, the Murano, and all those sparkling dregs of life in Memphis. She'd hire this tugboat captain, she mused, and they'd load up the Jag on one of those barges down at McKellar Lake, then move out into the river, to the spot that was deepest for miles around, Bauxippi Bend, and dump the Jag and all the loot from the marriage into the channel.

That fantasy played over and over in her thoughts, rich in detail like the macabre deliberations of someone considering suicide.

In early September she phoned Julia again and tried for some of her old flamboyance in announcing that she and Kip had split up, but failed and began to cry. Julia was sympathetic and promised not to tell anybody, not even Doctor Teddy. As the conversation went on and as Skyler's tears subsided she managed to ask—casually, she hoped—exactly where in New Mexico did Perry hang out.

"Up around Ruidoso," Julia told her. "You remember I told you about Uncle Bates going out there? That weird pilgrimage before he died? He said he just went to the mountains, asked around, and everybody seemed to know Greywolf. See, Perry's with the Apaches. Or maybe it's the splinter group of Mescaleros, the peyote and pussy cult."

"Neat religion," Skyler managed.

"Anyway, Uncle Bates said Perry seemed to know he was coming. Like a premonition. Like it was fate."

Julia obviously believed half this stuff, Skyler knew, so she resisted sarcasm. But she was glad she phoned Julia and it allowed a new fantasy to work itself into her head, a trip to visit Perry. After that call she put the household items in storage and traded the Jaguar for a big Japanese 4x4 heavy with chrome.

When she drove across the downtown bridge heading west she knew she'd never see this town or river again. She also didn't know if she needed a spiritual fix or a consolation fuck and she didn't care if Cousin Perry—for old time's sake—or Greywolf in all his mystic splendor gave it to her.

It takes a lifetime to drive across Texas. For Skyler it was a long tacky stretch to Little Rock, and even tackier drive to Texarkana—billboards and barbecue shacks everywhere—then a million miles through the interchanges of Dallas, then somehow onward to Fort Worth, then into the middle of nowhere and not even halfway there.

She tried to think of people to call on the cell phone, but one by one vetoed them all. Near Sweetwater she dialed up Julia, but Doctor Teddy's arch and pious voice answered so she hung up.

By nightfall she crossed the time zone and entered a twilight of mesas and the cool high desert; her tears turned the highway into blurry liquid, so she pulled over to get herself in control. A highway sign pointed a place called the Loco Hills. And Kip invaded her thoughts like an occupying force, the enemy she loved, the one person who she had always imagined loved her back, and she didn't have a son or daughter or, for that matter, even a loyal dog. She stood outside her vehicle—made for climbing straight up the sides of the mountain—and watched the stars come out. An odor of sage and a tinge of autumn rode the night air.

When her tears dried on her face it felt old and cracked like one of those dusty arroyos on the landscape.

At last she reached Roswell, checked into a Ramada Inn, and tried to sleep. She had only a bottle of expensive Pouilly-Fuissé and no corkscrew, so she burrowed into the bedclothes, her knees drawn up in the fetal position, hugging her legs more for consolation than comfort. Julia is my only true friend, she thought to herself, and I'll phone her in a few days. After I find Perry. After whatever happens.

At noon the next day she drove into Cloudcroft: the mountains all around, the pines murmuring to her, the swollen creeks billowing white underneath the highway bridges. She asked first at a wayside general store with old skis and wooden snowshoes tacked to its walls. Later she found a forest ranger standing beside his pickup truck on the side of the road.

"Who?" he asked, grinning. He was an awkward man, a smoker, ill at ease with himself.

"Greywolf," she repeated. "At least he calls himself that, but he's really my cousin Perry."

"You might ask at tribal headquarters or at the Bureau of Indian Affairs in Ruidoso," he suggested, then he wanted to talk about her big vehicle, its gas mileage and all that. As he went on she had a mini-fantasy about him, wondering if he wanted to take her up to his fire tower, up a high ladder to a room that smelled of cedar and tobacco smoke where he'd strip off her clothes and give her some sort of official inspection.

Later she pulled into a campground filled with Winnebagos, Airstreams, and a docile geriatric set who gave her blank stares.

In the village of Mescalero, nothing.

In Ruidoso: nothing at the Bureau, nothing in a souvenir shop filled with ugly turquoise, nothing in the coffee shop with a giant fake waterfall where she ordered a cheeseburger, but didn't eat it.

That night she checked into the Holiday Inn, lying awake to be haunted by memories, mostly about boys back in Austin: the one who stripped off her wet bathing suit and warmed her body with his own sunburned skin, the one who wanted only her mouth, the one for whom she never wore panties. She suffered a wanton teenage lust, as strong as any horny boy's, she remembered, and she had great legs, a long torso, and adequate breasts, and she easily melted when a boy showed at least minimal intelligence and a willingness to take her on. Then Kip: romantic sex kept them together and excited for years and years, then honeymoon and marriage ended simultaneously, so that now, lying in bed with the TV blinking at her, she still had this yearning, this dreadful yearning that could only be erotic desire—only that, right?—and she wanted to thrust herself into a new life, lifting her hips as if to receive a strange presence. Enter me, do it, she commanded that grim little hotel room, but when her memory started up again, Kip was always her lover. She went to the lavatory and splashed her face with cold water. Memory was a bad drug, a downer, and the past had to be blotted out, she told the cracked mirror, but easier said than done.

For three more days she retraced that same mountain highway, going between Cloudcroft and Ruidoso over those eerie passes, asking everyone the same question. The days turned cool, a north wind rattling the leaves of the aspens, the threat of winter coming, and by this time maybe Perry had gone for the season. Thinking that, her emotions waylaid her again—I'm late, too late—and tears blinded her. Bur after another almost sleepless night she drove out again, wanting breakfast. She stopped at a Shell station with a mini-mart and small café attached.

Sitting in a plastic booth overlooking the parking lot and an old dumpster she ordered eggs, toast, and coffee from a woman in a red wig. And there, exhausted, she gave up. The search, she realized, had come to an end.

The adjoining mini-mart offered a few items of atrocious Indian art: blankets of primary colors, pretentious R.C. Gorman prints, and some lopsided pottery. Having given up the search, she was already deciding where to go next. Julia, she told herself. Doctor Teddy will be gone before long and Julia will be much more disoriented than she imagines. I'll go down to Austin and see Julia.

A movement outdoors caught her attention: a man stood in the rusted metal dumpster tossing cardboard onto the pavement of the parking lot. She watched cardboard boxes floating down, then turned her gaze toward the man. A buckskin shirt. A ponytail, gray. Then the unmistakable profile: her cousin Perry, windblown, appearing on the cue of destiny, studying the trash around his feet.

She went outside, walked to the middle of the nearly vacant parking lot, and waited for him to notice her. When he did she was crying again and feeling that deep rupture inside.

Clumsily, raking his shin, he climbed out of the dumpster.

When he came and took her hands in his, she was bawling— and he knew. Later, thinking back on it, she understood that he had just followed the logic of seeing her there, but at the time he seemed magical, a mind reader.

"Kip left you," he said in the most matter of fact way.

She nodded and blubbered.

"Come on," he said, leading her, and they went to his big four wheeler, shiny and new, a blue Mercedes monster, and in spite of her hysteria she wondered how he could afford it. But now she was his: breakfast abandoned, her own vehicle left in its parking space, thoughts obliterated.

They drove along the highway for only a mile or so, then turned down a logging road into a dank valley. A cloudy, sullen day: mist shrouded the pines and rocky slopes. They passed a coil of immense chains, a pile that resembled some prehistoric beast at rest, then forded a narrow stream. He asked her how long she had been searching for him and she answered with a halting, child-like wheeze, trying to get her voice and thoughts under control.

Down and down: a valley of sharp hairpin turns.

From the limb of an aspen hung a strange bundle of feathers tied with beaded leather strands.

In the meadow a small metallic trailer waited, a circle of stones near its door, a wisp of smoke rising from the last embers of a fire. As he helped her out of the Mercedes she heard a bird call—such a forlorn sound that tears welled up in her eyes again. She found herself trembling under his touch as he guided her to a stone bench before that circle of stone.

"Here, please," he said gently, and he tossed a few sticks onto the embers and sat beside her. He took both her hands in his. Stroking the fingers, he asked her not to speak, not to tell him anything more about her troubles.

Silence followed. The bird's call this time was like a lute, distant and melodic, then silence came again.

He went on caressing her fingers as if pulling the pain out of their tips.

"We're going away," he began slowly. "That's what the boxes are for. Packing up. As I think I told you, I leave the mountains around this time every year and go down to the Baja Peninsula. I knew somebody was coming to see me, though, and I'm glad we didn't miss each other."

We, he said, and she answered to herself: yes, I'll go with you, take me to some warm beach, I'm ready.

His attention to her fingers calmed her.

Meanwhile a small flame leapt up from the embers.

"You've made a long journey and you're tired out, but you've already arrived at a kind of wisdom," he went on. "You're already wise, Skyler, believe me, no, don't protest. Just listen to me."

She felt like a fool, not at all wise.

Yet her fingers glowed with a warmth that moved up her arms and she couldn't look beyond his dark eyes.

"The reason you're coming to wisdom," he went on, "is because you've had a good mentor. Kip has shown you the world and you've opened your eyes and seen it. So you can always love Kip for this. And if he betrayed you it's because he hasn't grown enough to take the next step in life—and we can pity him for that—but he's done you a favor. He's thrown you out into a world, Skyler, that he actually prepared you to see."

"That's true," she admitted. He still did that wonderful thing to her fingers.

He told her to live in the present. "Everything is in the past," he said softly. "All the hurt and turmoil, and you've moved into a time when nobody can hurt you anymore, where you'll never be taken by surprise and you'll be comfortable with your fate. You're going to be free from the appetites that have owned you, Skyler, and you're going to be good humored about losing them."

She listened carefully, deciding that it was all true, so very true, spiritual even, and cockeyed. She started to ask about sex—always her preoccupation, strength, and weakness—then decided he'd just covered that.

Also, a certainty arrived: his massage was working wonders and for the first time in weeks she felt relaxed and, curiously, hungry again.

He was doing a good job of being Greywolf. You know who you are, you've always known, but now the suffering has added wisdom and you don't need others to fulfill your destiny. His whole recitation seemed sincere and she somehow wanted to comfort him in his efforts.

During this a woman came out of the trailer: older with coiffed white hair, dressed in Ralph Lauren's finest, smiling, and clearly in charge. Skyler knew instantly this was the owner of the big Mercedes. The woman strolled over and stood beside Perry, waiting until he finished talking with her arms folded across her thin frame. Her nails had been done recently: pale blue like her expensive denim shirt.

"Minta," Perry said, finally, with an odd formality, "this is my cousin Skyler. Skyler, this is Minta."

The two women regarded one another, then Minta began gathering the empty cardboard boxes from the rear of the Mercedes. As she went back inside the trailer with the boxes a sudden and complete intuition came to Skyler: Minta had lots of money, probably a neat condo down in Baja, and was undoubtedly Perry's current squeeze. Even more: she was educated, very bright, probably two or three times divorced, and a tolerant follower of whatever cult Perry had devised for himself out here in the woods.

Grinning with this new knowledge Skyler tried to listen to Perry's modulated voice once more, then saw that he held out an object to her. "This is your medicine pouch," he announced. "And, see, look, I'm putting your wedding ring inside it."

While stroking her fingers he had slipped off her ring. The little leather pouch decorated with embroidery and beadwork accepted her four-carat ring, then he closed the drawstrings. "What's inside this medicine pouch will be your secret and mine," he told her. "But keep it with you. It contains a few important seeds, maybe something to amuse you, and things for you to think about. On the outside of the pouch, here, see, that's the North Star, so you'll never be lost. Even if you don't believe in the supernatural, Skyler, this'll be lucky for you. Here, take it."

A little laugh came out of her as she accepted it.

"Perry, Honey, you're something," she said.

"And I've got to get moving, but hold on a second," he told her, and he went to the door of the trailer, knocked, and called out. "Minta? Honey, I'm driving Skyler back to the Shell station! Be right back, okay?"

They hoisted themselves back into the Mercedes.

"How're you feeling?" he asked, as they moved out.

"Really okay," she replied, and she did. She put her hands to her face and felt their warmth.

"I hate to hurry you, but we've just gotta get on the road today ourselves," he explained, and she watched his handsome profile as he steered them back up the logging road. That buckskin shirt or his, she decided, undoubtedly a gift from Minta, must have cost hundreds of dollars—probably out of the Sundance catalog.

As he drove Perry began talking about logging on government land, making some sort of environmental statement, but she wasn't fully listening anymore.

At the Shell station and mini-mart she rather hoped he might kiss her, but he kept their goodbye reverential. He did take her hands in his once more to say that spiritual journeys were always, well, successful.

After he drove off she went into the little café and found the woman in the wig who said, "Lordy, Honey, where'd you go? We almost called the state troopers!"

"I'd still like breakfast," Skyler said. "But with sausage. Lots of sausage, links or patties or whatever you've got."

"We saw you drive off with that guy who was in the dumpster," said the waitress, leaning against the booth.

"He's my cousin. And it's a long story."

"You had us worried. And, listen, I'm gonna have the cook scramble up some fresh eggs. I'll just toss these out, no charge."

The woman gave Skyler a look of understanding and kindness as she went off with the old breakfast, a benevolent glance that only women share. After this Skyler dumped the contents of the medicine pouch on the plastic table and poked through its contents: her ring, a pair of dice, seeds, a sliver of turquoise, a tiny ball of fur, a couple of pine needles, a feather, a half moon of somebody's fingernail, and a shard of rose colored glass.

The waitress came back with a mug of hot coffee.

"See, what bothered cook and me was this," she told Skyler. "This guy is scrounging around in our dumpster and you drive off with him, leavin' your car and breakfast. On the other hand he's drivin' that new Mercedes wagon. We didn't have any idea he was your cousin."

"Perry turned himself into an Indian medicine man and calls himself Greywolf," Skyler said, sipping the coffee.

With that, the waitress sat down opposite her in the booth and they began talking about religion. The waitress wanted to know if somebody had to ordain an Indian medicine man. Eventually they began speculating about God.

"What bothers me," Skyler said, finishing her scrambled eggs, "is that if we're in God's image, then he's in ours. That makes him a greedy, self-serving, egotistical bastard like the rest of us."

"True," the waitress answered thoughtfully, tugging at the curls of her wig. "I never even considered that."

That afternoon Skyler drove eastward. She didn't know exactly where she was going, but she supposed she'd stop and see Julia in Austin. Julia, she told herself, was funny as hell. Also mystical.

Texas Heat

Carla met him first: an oddly handsome, tall, grinning cowboy type with large red hands. He introduced himself as Boomer Smith and said he grew up in Harlingen and the Valley, but moved around these days chasing deals. He wanted a nice house out in the Hill Country, he said, with a pool, a view, and, if possible, stables.

Carla told her partner, Mary Beth, about him. They owned a small realty company, Lantana, out on Highway 290, west of Austin, and specialized in small ranches.

"He bring a letter from a bank?" Mary Beth asked. "He sounds too good to be true."

"Said he'd pay cash. But he also said we could check his credit, though I haven't done it. I think we're talking a buyer who'll spend a million or two."

"You like him?"

"Kinda. Once or twice this look came over his face, though."

"What sort of look?"

"Like he definitely might want to get in my pants."

"Carla, we're having a lousy month and you know it. You might have to sacrifice your body."

"Tell me about it," Carla answered, and they shared a snort of laughter.

Mary Beth and Carla decided in college that they could run a successful real estate business together, but since that time they had suffered failed marriages, money problems, heartbreaks, and heavy competition from the larger real estate firms in both Austin and over in Blanco County. They struggled to pay rent on their office building, a washed-out abode with noisy plumbing set back in a grove of scrub oaks and wind-blown mesquite trees halfway out toward Dripping Springs. Mary Beth had a nine-year-old son with asthma, Luke, who sat on the bench for his Little League team and Carla had a demanding mother with too many cats and a series of bad hairdressers who cut too much off. Even so, both Carla and Mary Beth danced the salsa at Miguel's, the Texas Two Step at the Broken Spoke, and up close on Sixth Street with assorted telephone linemen, executives, former halfbacks and dull professors. They traded date notes after occasions at Threadgill's or The Oasis and agreed on just one general rule between them: no musicians.

They also took care. At the clubs or in business they worried about men.

When they met male clients at isolated houses or ranch property they went as a team, a caution against unwanted sexual advances. They vowed to watch out for each other, figuring they lived in a masculine ethos: beer and barbeque, football and bullshit, kisses and violence.

Boomer Smith, of course, had a shy, goofy, awkward way about him and wouldn't even meet their gaze. Carla felt motherly toward him because his Stetson was somehow tilted wrong and he moved clumsily, bumping chairs and desks with his hip, fumbling, grinning, and getting out of sync even in his best moments.

"How can he go around making deals? He hardly talks!" Mary Beth observed while they waited to show him the first property.

"Maybe he does all right with the guys," Carla offered. "He was probably the nerdy valedictorian in high school. Straight A's and a member, you know, of the model airplane club."

He arrived an hour late after their part-time secretary, Maria, had gone home for the day. Held up at the Driskill Hotel, he told them, and very sorry. He brought them each a single rose and offered to take them to dinner as compensation, but still wouldn't look directly at either of them.

They drove out to a small ranch near Driftwood. On the way Mary Beth asked if he meant to raise cattle and he said, "No, maybe horses," yet he admitted he didn't ride. Carla asked if he had a family and he said, "No, I'm single and mean to stay that way." He snapped off that last reply, so that five minutes of silence ensued. Later, the little ranch looked overgrown and wrong.

"Maybe if you could give us an idea of how much you intend to spend," Carla ventured cautiously. "I mean, if this place is just too small, what do you have in mind?"

"I mean to impress," he instructed them, and that cryptic reply—as they later discussed with one another—was curiously worded and spoken. His voice actually changed when he said it. The drawl vanished. He seemed more out of place than ever, a lost outsider employing a strangely arch diction.

At The Salt Lick, though, a big barbecue hangout on a nearby farm road, they relaxed. Boomer bought a case of Budweiser, laughed for the first time, and began to tell stories one about his mother, who lived near Alpine and owned a pet kangaroo, and another about an uncle who lived in a maze of trailers in the middle of nowhere near Amarillo. In such tales his drawl returned and he became an affable and earnest country boy.

"Six trailers," he said about his uncle's place. "Two of 'em big double-wides. Lashed together with cable, so they won't blow off in a dust storm!" In their accompanying laughter they forgave him his peculiarities and he fit, clearly, Carla's view of him as a former high school nerd, the one with the nutty family, the one who never knew what to do with his hands. While they ate peach cobbler and pecan pie with their coffee, later, Mary Beth went on about her little boy, Luke, who didn't fit in at school and who occasionally whined that he wanted to live with his drunken daddy. Boomer offered that Mary Beth seemed practical and sure of herself and that she could undoubtedly accomplish more with him than any man. When she smiled at this flattery he went on, saying, that a young boy needs his mother, ask any psychologist, and if the teenager, later, needed a stronger hand, then maybe the father. "But for now, Mary Beth, have confidence in your intuitions," and he placed a big red hand over hers as big, moist, inebriated tears appeared in her eyes.

"I think Boomer's just wonderful," Mary Beth said, turning suddenly to Carla, who watched all this over the rim of her coffee cup.

"He's fine," Carla replied. "But when you drink beer, Mary Beth, you have a tendency to fall in love, to believe in gurus, or to want plastic surgery."

Minutes later they reeled through the parking lot arm in arm beneath a gaudy display of stars in a moonless sky. Boomer forgot his Stetson, so Mary Beth volunteered to retrieve it, leaving Carla alone with him. She leaned against the rail fence and gazed up at the Milky Way—a down-home name for a galaxy, she commented—and Boomer moved beside her. For a moment she thought he might try to kiss her, and then she wondered if he intended to say something, but he remained wordless and didn't make a move. When Mary Beth came back wearing the Stetson down over her ears and grinning, he moved off sideways, awkwardly, in retreat. They were soon all talking at once and driving back.

A few days went by. Clients materialized, including a young couple with only a thousand dollars for a down payment. When Boomer phoned again, Carla told him about a spread at the edge of Blanco County, a working horse ranch whose owners agreed to let him look at it. No, he said, he didn't want to deal with occupants, not with anybody except Carla and Mary Beth themselves.

"Maybe you can drive by the ranch and look at it," Carla suggested. "I'll give you directions. If you like it, we'll arrange to see it when the owners are away."

He agreed.

But he also said that he had business in Galveston, so another week passed before they heard from him again.

Carla lived in an apartment just off the Mopac: four big rooms furnished with light pine furniture and lots of gadgets—an espresso machine, an ice cream maker, a big music center, a 41-inch TV, and dozens of novelty clocks, mobiles, and sculptures that turned on rotating pedestals. That week she and Mary Beth attended another Little League game, watching Luke sit in the dugout, then play right field after the score was decided. Afterward, walking away from the concession stand, Carla thought she saw Boomer's big dark Lincoln Continental, and she walked halfway across the parking lot to make sure. It was somebody else's car. Later, she fretted over the mistake.

When Boomer came back he gave Carla a friendship ring. Just an item bought in Galveston, he said, but it was too extravagant: a sapphire of about a half carat. "Payment for all the work you've been doing," he said, and he gently pushed away her hand when she tried to give it back.

"To tell the truth, I bought it second-hand," he admitted, not looking at her. "It was a genuine bargain. You take it. Please."

They were at the office on Maria's day off. Carla had been typing out a contract for the young couple, who were probably going to be turned down by loan officers. The toilet down the hallway made an embarrassing noise.

"Did you drive over and look at that ranch in Blanco County?" Carla asked, trying the ring on her finger. It was a dazzling gift, bigger than the wedding ring she once wore, and she couldn't analyze the nervousness she felt.

"Didn't go by," he said of the ranch in question. "But I saw another place over that way. Just off Highway 165. A vacant house that looks new with good grassland."

"I'll find out who handles it and set up an appointment," she told him, and at that point Mary Beth and Luke drove up, the windshield of her green Toyota flashing at them. Carla felt strange and caught, especially moments later when she showed Mary Beth the ring and tried to explain why she couldn't accept it, yet had. Boomer hunched down and talked to Luke while Carla followed Mary Beth back to the toilet, where they jiggled the handle, grinned, gave each other looks, and tried to cope with their client.

"It's just an inappropriate gift," Carla said of the ring. "What do you suppose he thinks it means?"

"Honey, accept it," Mary Beth advised. "When he chooses a house, we'll sell the damn thing and split the profit as part of our commission."

"He wants to get me in bed, I just know it," Carla sighed.

"Well, sure he does. You're a looker and he's clumsy as a goose. He didn't know what to do, so he just bought that damn ring."

When they emerged, Boomer was showing Luke how to throw a curve ball and, somehow, baseball made everything natural again. Mary Beth actually flirted, bumping Boomer with her hip, and they all grinned and went out for burgers. At the Dairy Dip, Boomer played pinball and, later, showed Luke a switchblade knife with a curved ivory handle, but something happened so that Luke came over with his root beer float and sat beside his mother as if he didn't want anything more to do with Boomer.

"What happened, Honey?" Mary Beth asked, but Luke wouldn't respond.

"Did Boomer hurt your feelings?" Carla persisted, but Luke just crushed his baseball cap in his fist—a pinstripe cap in the New York Yankees style—and sucked the straw of his empty root beer float. Meanwhile, Boomer slapped the sides of the pinball machine, his face and raw hands illumined in its glow.

"What, Luke? Tell me," his mother kept on.

"Oh it's some male conspiracy thing," Carla decided, so they let it go.

The weekend arrived and Carla continued to fret. It was illegal to run a credit report, but she considered it. She didn't want to ask Boomer to allow himself to be investigated because she might offend him and lose a sale. Too awkward, she told herself, yet her skepticism annoyed her, especially since she had accepted the ring. She scolded herself for having doubts.

The weather turned hotter.

According to the listing information, the house out on 165 had sixteen adjoining acres, no pool, no stable, and no view, but Boomer wanted to see it that weekend, so Carla made arrangements. Mary Beth would attend another Little League game with Luke, Carla would show another house to the young couple with only a thousand dollars, then they would meet Boomer out in the hill country late on Saturday.

A wind blew up, but hot: swirls of dust in the flats, trees bending on the ridges, great pavilions of cloud rising on the southern zephyrs. Deadly humidity, too: Carla's blouse stuck to her back and the young couple perspired and whined. She wanted Boomer to write a big fat check, so she could go off to the mountains, up in New Mexico, say, where the nights turned cold even in summertime.

She drove west behind an old slow pickup and couldn't pass in the traffic, then turned off on a farm road quivering with a mirage of rising heat. The twang of an irritating guitar jangled her nerves, so she turned off the radio.

Following another realtor's instructions she found the house: an angular rock, cypress, and glass monstrosity—no architect would do such a thing—along a dry creek bed in a stand of live oak and cottonwood trees. The house could barely be seen from the highway and she wondered how Boomer had found it, but there he was, waiting, leaning against his big Continental beside a rock archway and gate, grinning and waving. He had sweated through his T-shirt and his Stetson was pushed back on his head.

"Found me," he said, as Carla got out of her car.

"Lordy, I feel like I've driven all day," she managed in reply, and she manufactured a smile. The heat bore down on them.

"The house is already open," Boomer told her. "I peeked inside."

With that they started up the flagstone walkway. She felt relieved to be rid of the young couple and confident that Mary Beth and Luke would soon be along.

"You know, I like this place," he said when they stood in the living room.

"Nice," Carla agreed, though she didn't completely mean it.

The high windows let in a brass colored and stifling heat of late afternoon.

"It's nothing like I wanted," he admitted. "But it has a good feel to it."

"This happens a lot," she said, as they made their way toward the kitchen. "A client will have a very specific idea about what he wants, then buy something completely different. Just goes to show."

"I'm not anybody's usual client," Boomer reminded her, and his voice did that thing again: formality crept in an aloof arch tone.

"No, I don't want to imply that you are. You're one of a kind, Boomer, really, I mean it."

"Hey, you're not wearing the ring."

"It's in my purse. I intend to have it sized right away."

They admired the kitchen and breakfast nook decorated with bright Mexican tiles, then they stepped outside on the wide deck across the back of the house. At one corner of the deck an outdoor shower surrounded by glass brick emptied into a drain that led through the cottonwood grove to the dry creek. Boomer stepped inside the shower and found that the water could be turned on.

"Look at this! Nice, huh?"

"It's a great outdoor shower," Carla agreed.

"Tell you what. Let's take a shower and cool off."

"You go ahead," she managed, and that nervous laugh came out of her. Before she knew it, he began to skin out of his T-shirt and sat down abruptly on a wooden bench to remove his boots.

"Now come on, don't leave," he instructed her. "At least stand guard, so Mary Beth doesn't barge in on me." He had a wide grin and as he fumbled with his belt his effort seemed frantic, childlike, as though his big hands couldn't keep up with his enthusiasm.

She watched until he began to stumble around in his jeans, trying to get them off, then she turned away, laughing, and thinking, no, you're certainly not the usual client, you're a doofus, you're too much, and she caught a glimpse of his bare butt as he entered the shower stall. Above the glass bricks, then, she could see his grinning face and the curve of the chrome shower head.

"Whoa!" he yelled when the water came on. "That's cold!"

"I'll bet it's nice," she called to him. He made a noise like a goat and ran his long fingers through his hair.

When she started to leave, he once again called her back, saying, "You know, I think I'll buy this place. I'd have to add a stable, but it could be small. I only intend to keep a coupla horses."

She found herself getting used to this silliness of his: talking business while buck naked underneath a shower.

"You haven't even seen the upstairs," she reminded him.

"Five bedrooms, five baths, all tucked away, very private. I like it. You know, I think I'll make out a check."

She began to feel lightheaded. Cash, a solid commission. Then he started talking about an apartment in Austin, too: Something close to the center for nights he might want to stay in town. She sat down on the wooden bench while he yelled out his thoughts. Was there anything for sale around Town Lake? Some real nice condos?

"Carla, are you there?"

"Right here," she said, standing up again, so he could see her. "Standing guard as ordered."

"Just drape my T-shirt over the stall,' he said. "I'll dry with it. And if you don't mind, lay my jeans over the side, too."

While he dressed, she suggested that he should make a low bid on the house, but he rejected that. No, the asking price seemed fair, he said, and they went back to a discussion of condos. Maybe something around the university, he added. He liked to watch the kids come and go.

By the time he came out of the shower, dressed, they were laughing so naturally that when he suggested that she should hop into the cold water, too, she considered it.

"I won't watch, promise," he told her. "In fact, I'll go get a big ol' beach towel outta my car. I bought it in Galveston, never used it, and you can dry off with it afterward."

"Well, maybe," she allowed, and by now, somehow, all of Boomer's unpredictability was part of a general charm.

"We'll do it this way," he said. "Wait until I bring the towel to you, then I'll go away again. I'll go wait for Mary Beth and Luke and when you're finished you can show me upstairs. Or we can walk off some of the land. How about it?"

"Sounds okay," she agreed. "I'll wait for you."

He hurried off and while he was gone Carla listened to a dove's familiar call from the glade. The sun sank low behind the cottonwoods and the last of the wildflowers—so lush in the springtime that they blanketed the hillsides—now filled what remained of the day with their sweet decay. She wondered if someone like Boomer could possibly become her fate: an odd guy, never quite on cue. The money, of course, would make a difference, and she speculated for a moment about a life where sapphires came as easily as Cracker Jack prizes. Awkward endearments would be the routine, not romance, she knew, but romance never worked anyway. And she wanted somebody to love and care for; her mother had sensed the vacuum in her life, so had become too demanding and the only things that moved in her apartment were the mechanical sculptures. Such thoughts—and a chorus of dove calls from the darkening trees—occupied her until Boomer came back with the beach towel, grinned, shuffled his feet, backed away and excused himself.

"You just take your time," he assured her. "I'll be out front. When you're all done, you can show me the rest of the house."

After he disappeared she stripped off quickly, left her clothes draped over the stall, stepped in, and turned on the tap. A little shriek came out of her when the cold water hit her skin, then she stood there, getting used to it, and noting that the beach towel said *Welcome To Biloxi*, so that she wondered how Boomer came to buy such a thing in Galveston.

She wished she had soap. Then, holding her face up to the spray, her thoughts going nowhere in particular, she felt his arms encircle her.

"Boomer!" she cried out with another burst of nervous laughter. "You lied to me, you devil!" And to herself: Okay, here it is, deal with it, stupid, because you're bare-assed and helpless.

She spoke to him again, but he didn't answer and she could feel his naked body pressed against her backside, feel his chest rising and falling with excited breathing, and feel, distinctly, his pubic hair pressed against her hip. He turned her slightly, cupping a breast in his giant hand, saying nothing, and she felt him trembling as if all his timid wires had come loose.

A moment passed, then she said softly, "There, Boomer, steady," and she felt strangely motherly and helpful as if he hadn't deceived her, as if he hadn't circled back and slipped out of his clothes again. She took his free hand in hers and felt its shudder. For all his boldness he was sexually frightened, she sensed, and in this knowledge her own fear lessened.

"Boomer?" she murmured again, gently, urging him to say something. But he kept his silence. She knew she couldn't fully express in her apprehension: He had stepped over the line into this heavy sexual move, but couldn't go on. Dozens of times in her life Carla had experienced this, a sad thing, really: The aggressive mating male often boldly lurches forward into an embarrassing sexual paralysis and requires soothing out.

"Boomer? There, it's all right," she heard herself say.

"Very well," he said in rasp. And his voice became strangely formal again, clipped, the Texas drawl gone. "Touch me."

With this request—or was it a command?—she felt curiously in charge and decided to obey. As he bent forward, dipping his head into the stream of water so that his lips touched her shoulder, she let her fingers move down his body. He was limp and pitiful, nothing there at all, and she decided that the cold water pouring over them caused this, so began to lead him out of the stall. She even managed a smile and let him gawk at her nakedness, then she saw that her clothes were gone. "Boomer, Honey," she said gently and carefully, "where are my clothes?" and she managed to still keep her calm although this was definitely a little crazy.

"You're very pretty naked," he told her, and his voice was someone else who used considerably more proper diction. "I knew you would be."

"Here, let me get the towel," she said, and she pulled it off the stall as he led her by the hand. They padded across the deck, leaving wet footprints, passing through the tiled kitchen and into the den where he took the towel from her and spread it onto the plush carpet. Fine, alright, he's gaining confidence, she told herself, and we're going to do it now, okay, and she thought about her sexual history—how many boys and men? Fifteen? A husband and two lovers of some duration and all the others—and she decided that she hadn't been promiscuous, not really, maybe it was sixteen or twenty, it was the way of the world, the adventure and the desperation, and she settled on the towel and pulled Boomer down beside her. Pressed against him, she could still feel his indecisiveness so she tried to kiss him—to say, yes all right, with a kiss—but he wouldn't have it.

And where was Mary Beth? And the only sounds now were the distant three-part notes of the dove and his labored breathing, that deep rasp, and he turned her on her side and settled himself against her thigh and began grinding himself against her, so that she thought, no, wait, should I help him out here? And from his mouth came a deep sound, an unexpected, doleful, creepy subtext to his breathing: "Nnnnn, Nnnnn." She felt her lower lip tremble and knew she might cry, but held on.

He had no erection, but moved against her thigh in a wild impersonation of the act, and she felt her heart go out to him even as she wanted to weep for herself. She prayed to the wall, oh, God, please, don't let him be the one, and she didn't even know what she meant, exactly, but the prayer spilled out of her along with a sob. She clasped her hand over her mouth, so he wouldn't hear her cry, and his movement went on and on, accompanied by that same "Nnnnn," that he made with his teeth clenched and in what seemed to be a prolonged agony that he couldn't release.

At last something in him was finished and he lay beside her, his arm draped across her ribcage, and she fought for control, trying to recover, until finally she managed to say, "Boomer? If it's all right now, I'd like to get my clothes. Where are they? You can tell me now." And she spoke to him as if he were a child, she realized, with a parent's calm, but it didn't sound right, he wasn't stupid, she knew, and the condescension was unmistakable.

"Go look out that window," he told her evenly with his strange new voice.

"Which window?"

"That one in front of you. Tell me what you see."

She got to her feet, wrapping her arms around her breasts, and padded over to the window, bent and covering herself. The final slant of a red sunset touched the trees and for a moment the view comforted her.

"What?" she asked, looking out. "See what?"

He came and stood beside her.

"Here, put this on," he said, and she turned to see that he held the sapphire ring. Obediently, she allowed him to slip it on her index finger.

"There we are. My signature," he announced, smiling, and his voice, she decided, was like a trained actor's, a voice that could project or dive into a whisper and that knew exactly its effect.

"You're not from Texas, are you, Boomer?" she asked, and her own voice trembled with the question.

"Sure I am," he told her. "Same as the Bowie knife. Like the drought in summer or the blizzard in winter. A force of nature. Like the tornado. Like the rattlesnake and scorpion. Same as the blinding dust storm. That's exactly who I am and where I'm from."

It seemed like a practiced speech, one delivered by a curious foreigner, and although her mouth twitched involuntarily and although she wanted to bolt away she gazed out the window yet again to see the sun's last rays pick up something metallic in the hillside stand of cottonwoods. A car. It was out there in the woods. She looked more closely and knew this was what he had meant her to see. Somebody's car, green. And then she knew.

"Come on, we'll get your clothes," he told her, leading her away. She embraced his words in hopeless hope, wanting everything to be zany and perfectly all right, wanting Boomer to be the guy at the pinball machine, the big clumsy guy, but she knew better. The ring, she knew, had belonged to some woman before her. His signature. Prayers and memories fell on her, then, like weights.

He led her through the master bedroom to an enormous bathroom covered with the remains of Mary Beth and Luke. In a far corner, smeared with blood and casually tossed aside, was the pinstripe baseball cap, and why, she asked herself, why me? I don't deserve this, nobody does, I'm really a good person, a little lonely, trying hard, and he's not even named Boomer, he used somebody else's name, and I don't even believe he's from Texas, not at all, he's lying, he's not one of us.

Two Cars on a Hillside

There were eight of us and we all worked hard in our high school classes, played on the teams and kept things normal with outsiders, including our parents, so our secret stayed intact.

The girls were Dana, Sylvie, Joanna, and Tibby. The guys were Brad, Chase, Tim, and me. They called me Kipper in those days, a name that came out of the baseball squad, who knows what it meant? Even my father called me that after a while.

My father also seemed concerned about who my steady girl might be. One night at supper he started again, saying, "Okay, I think Dana's your best gal, am I right?"

"We're good friends," I answered. "You know, for the movies and ball games. We don't want to get too serious."

"That's perfectly smart of you," my mother put in.

"Well, true, you don't want anything complicated," my father admitted, drawing on his heavier baritone, the voice he sometimes used in town meetings.

"Real friendship is wonderful," said my mother. "You're all intelligent kids. Romantic love is probably a silly idea to you."

I nodded with relief. The roast beef that night was cooked rare, the best cut. We ate well at our house because my father owned the big market and butcher shop in our little Texas town. He was putting on weight that year, moving toward the heart attack that took him away.

"Can I use the delivery car again this weekend?" I asked that night.

"One accident or one ticket and you don't use it anymore," he reminded me always. I delivered groceries for my father's store, but we went through this ritual every weekend. Most of our group had driven ranch tractors or pickup trucks from the time we were thirteen years old, driving illegally, covering several counties around Dripping Springs, and our parents gave us permission—because of our good grades, our mainstream lives, our innocence.

At school the eight of us agreed there would be no meaningful glances between us, no touching, no bragging, no confessions if caught, and no falling in love with just one of the partners. Looking back, wondering how it all happened, I remember all the guys as slender and muscular. Both Dana and Joanna would become school queens although Sylvie and Tibby in their separate ways were even more stunning.

Things began the night we drove into Austin. Afterward, driving back from the movie, Chase and Tibby started undressing each other in the back seat. I gripped the wheel of the old Chevy, stunned, as Dana kept peering over at them and breaking into nervous laughter.

"You keep doin' that," she warned them, "and I'm gonna keep watching." She nudged me and jerked her head toward them, trying to get me to watch with her.

"They're in a trance!" she finally squealed, and she clawed at my shirt, urging me to stop the car and to become a spectator with her. After another mile I pulled into a roadside park, stopped, turned off the headlights, and turned around. By this time Tibby had shed the rest of her clothes and I found myself addled with the sight of her nakedness. Dana began to stroke my backside. Dumbstruck, empty of thought or language, I didn't know what more to do until Dana gently moved against me, making her own signals clear. Then as I started unbuttoning her denim shirt I thought, hey, this is it, we're all virgins, but this is it. This is ignition. Then the endowment inside her bra filled up my puny imagination.

Chase made deep growling noises.

It was a moonless April evening: the hawks silent in the scrub oaks, the fields alive with the smells of earth and sage.

"Go ahead, touch me there," Dana whispered, and the car became hot with movement and starglow. We opened the car doors that faced a mesquite grove and a cluster of cedars. As Dana and I began our awkward contortions, Chase and Tibby reached a loud crescendo. In a few moments they leaned forward over the seat to become our grinning audience. We all became exhibitionists in our first couplings, oblivious, proud of our bodies, part of the wonder of the night, mysterious and reckless.

As I met and received Dana's rhythmic thrusts she arched herself, reaching up, her heavy breasts flattened, stretching out as if in a delicious yawn, and found Chase in her arms. They kissed in a long, delirious, wanton hello as I found Tibby's eyes fixed in mine. A capricious tick of the psychological clock in us all: Tibby held out her hand and I took it. The girls passed one another as they climbed over the car seat, then we all groaned and started again. Tibby's slender body became a new intoxicant and she moved against me like an oiled and experienced woman.

Half an hour later we stood and sat outside the car, naked, cooling ourselves, our thoughts obliterated. Chase, our quarterback, our first baseman, the friend who worked in my father's grocery store at my side, leaned against the old Chevy with his muscular arms folded across his chest, a two hundred pound god, serene, as if the night belonged to him. I sat on the fender with my arms around both girls, listening: I could hear the wheeling of the stars overhead, the cosmic winds, mortal voices from other planets, and I felt both drained and wise.

Occasionally a car passed on the highway. Tibby addressed us in that throaty voice of hers. She was our intellectual, the debate squad member, a writer of notebooks that no one was ever allowed to read, and she was musing on what had just happened, yet in that special way of hers. "Now I'm sixteen and one hour old," she sighed, and I loved her deep world-weary voice.

Then a car cruised up beside us in the darkness and stopped. It happened with Tibby's sighing observation covering the sound of the approaching tires. Arriving with its headlights off, it was there with us before we had a chance to be startled, so we were naked, philosophical, and caught.

"Kipper?" asked a voice, and it was Brad. The old Dodge had entered the familiar roadside park in darkness, its occupants looking for a spot to make out, and they recognized my mottled white Chevy—the delivery car with its license plates forever tilted.

"Chase?" came the soft whisper of a girl's voice.

The faces of Brad, Tim, Sylvie, and Joanna peered at us and we heard our names repeated in shocked amusement. Looking back, though, it was Chase who made the difference. He stood

61

there as indifferent as a marble statue, beautiful and muscular, his penis still swollen, arms crossed, and only later did Joanna and Sylvie admit to what desire, jealousy, and yearning they suddenly felt. I wanted to cover myself, but Tib and Dana stood their ground, so there I was: trapped in the naked tableau, seeing the gesture through, taking my unspoken instructions to stay cool. In any case Sylvie decided that we wouldn't outdo her. She slid out of the car, raised her arms, and pushed her fingers into her dark hair. For a moment she struck that dancer's pose, legs slightly apart in an arrogant stance. Then she somehow reached back and drew her cotton dress straight up and over her head. She wasn't wearing a bra and she came out of her panties in a neat, liquid movement. No one said anything.

Twenty years ago, all this.

Our town was small then and now, not yet developed into a bedroom community for nearby Austin, and our families lived in the smug values of times maybe thirty years before that time, in years that hardly seemed touched by assassinations, Vietnam, or any part of the sexual revolution. The middle of Texas: we grew up on church suppers, sports, fair play, and honest labor. Our houses stood up white and pious, part of a stubborn theology of a time that had actually passed away.

What set the eight of us apart in those strange days? We experimented a little with booze, sure, but found it ineffective and stupid compared to the inebriations of the flesh. None of us were radicals. We liked each other because we were all psychologically straight without annoying tics or dark corners. Tibby, later, in one of her more thoughtful moments, offered that it was the movies we went to see. We did love movies. So into our consciousness came Michael Corleone, Sally Bowles, James Bond, the shark from Jaws, Woody Allen, Peter Sellers, and a hundred couples who talked dirty and did it onscreen. Locked in the middle of the continent, we were hooked on the big screens, popcorn, and the exotic worlds beyond Texas. We became free, Tibby suggested, because life was out there to be seen, instructing us, daring us with all the images that began to take inside us.

"You want to drive into Austin for what? I didn't even know they made Australian movies," said my father one evening. "And I can't believe the parents of those girls put up with your late hours, either."

"We just see a movie, go for burgers, and talk, that's all we ever do," I argued. "Nobody drinks. We drive slow. All the other parents trust us."

That won my mother to my side again. "We trust you, too," she insisted. "But do try to be home a little earlier."

After a ballgame with Lampasas—I played shortstop, got a hit, and Chase whacked a homer—we drove to the hillside at the far end of Brad's daddy's ranch. We could see for miles from that little hillside, so could easily spot the headlights of any approaching car. This was soon after our first meeting, but already our inhibitions had vanished in a barrage of dirty talk and sexual acrobatics. We all wanted each other. We gave anatomy lessons, howling with laughter or groaning in unison. Blankets and pillows appeared. Hygiene and the use of the pill became topics and it became a frenzied class, night class, we called it, and there were few rules. One night we played hide and seek, but that proved uncomfortable—too many thorns and stickers in the Texas night. Tim, who was the loudest among us, soon settled down, and after the sex we soon started settling into one car, crowding together to talk. The subjects ranged from life on other planets to the dreary lives or our parents. Also Dracula. Mick Jagger. Religion. And bums who took drugs.

I was the astronomy freak and out there beneath the stars where the heavens opened up to us we talked about the speed of light, the formation of the galaxies, and the nature of infinity—the concept, we decided, beyond concepts. It was teenage excitement and speculation: only a few random facts, but intense.

"Black holes suck," Tim offered wistfully, like a line of melancholy wisdom, and we broke into laughter.

There was a night toward the end of the school year when, after sex, exhausted, the girls sat in the Dodge discussing Warren Beatty and the guys slumped in the Chevy talking sports.

Then, later, we decided who would take whom to the prom. I asked for Tibby because I figured she'd keep up the conversation all evening. Other classmates invited various ones of us to drag race over at Marble Falls or to go skinny dipping or to take part in a special breakfast over at The Salt Lick, but we all knew what we wanted when the official ceremonies ended: we wanted to be back on the hillside folding silken dresses and rented tuxedoes into the trunks of the cars, going at each other again.

On prom night we had the first of several fantasy sessions. In time, we played doctors and nurses, bosses and secretaries, and models and photographers. We felt ourselves changing, yet couldn't say how. Our lives were the same, yet not.

That summer all of the guys and two of the girls worked part-time while Chase and I played summer league baseball. We still kept our dates on the hillside, but complications set in. Two yeast infections. Then Sylvie was grounded for yelling at her mother, though her parents forgave her in four days. The carburetor in the Dodge went out and Tim's parents promised to fix it, but didn't. We found a rebuilt one and struggled to install it down at the mini-mart at the town's only stoplight.

One day Tibby, who worked mornings in the gift shop, brought me a book on astronomy. Blurry telescope photos, mostly, and a few artist's conceptions that are now long outdated. The birth of the stars, all that. I was loading up cardboard boxes for my noon deliveries when she stopped off. We stood beside the meat locker in the store as Chase, sweeping the floor, gave us a knowing glance, raising an eyebrow as if to say, hey, no flirting.

Tibby asked me if I wanted her to make deliveries with me.

"What for?" I asked, being dumb.

"Just to do it, okay?"

"Sure, I guess so," I answered, and I looked over to see if Chase was still watching us.

"Then I'll wait in the Chevy," she said lightly, and she went off toward the front of the store with a nice sway, waving at my father before she went out the door. She would circle back to the car in the alley, I knew, and the deception gave me a charge.

"You two got something up?" Chase asked, coming over with his broom. He wasn't smiling.

"Nah, everything's cool," I told him, and I showed him the book and explained why she stopped by, lying to my best friend, yet it was a lie in the future tense, a lie of possibilities and uncertainties.

Tibby and I made two deliveries in town, then took a back road out toward the Grandy ranch way over on the Blanco River. While the car took the curves on the road, Tibby pulled up her knees and hugged them against herself. She talked about how in a year or so she'd be at UT studying, then how in two years after that she'd take a junior year abroad, traveling around Europe, and how she planned to be a journalism major, then a writer even better than an ordinary journalist, not that she knew exactly what sort. As we drove I glanced at her long legs, the most perfect long legs. She was like a movie librarian, one of those who suddenly takes off her glasses and lets down her hair to reveal that she's really the most beautiful girl in the movie, not just some dog librarian. Seriously good looking. Tim said that about her, once, but added that she was also seriously and unfortunately smart.

Driving along as she talked, I thought how I watched her that first night at the roadside park. In a corner of my thoughts she was Chase's girl because they started it all. So why did she ask to come with me today? And what was I feeling?

The summer grew suddenly more complex.

She carried one of the two boxes of groceries onto the porch of the ranch house where Mrs. Grandy met us. We were led inside the old rock house where the old man sat drooling on his wheelchair in a room filled with bric-a-brac, doilies, musty rugs and creaky furniture. We accepted a sugar cookie warm from the oven. Small talk. Tibby asked all the right questions about the old man's condition and said all the appropriate things, but, meanwhile, waiting for the rest of the afternoon to reveal itself, I felt my chest tighten so I couldn't breathe.

We waved goodbye and drove away. Near the river we found a bower of live oaks and a curtain of thick cedar trees that blocked the view from the road, hiding us. The strong midsummer fragrance of the river filled the car.

"Let's do oral," Tibby said, grinning wickedly. As I turned off the engine I could only look ahead at the swirling waters of the river and nod. It was something the eight of us had never done and I wasn't sure, for my part, how to go about it.

She kissed me, later, with my own taste in her mouth, a kiss like nothing I had ever known, possessive and softly fierce. She was breathing hard, laughing, and saying, "Oh god, that's a first, oh my," and I felt unusually successful in my performance, joining in her laughter.

Afterward we started talking again. I suggested that we should maybe put our clothes on and I had the overpowering desire to get out of there, but she went on about writing and traveling the world.

"C'mon," I urged her. "Somebody might come along. It's the middle of the day."

She might become a novelist, she told me, or a foreign correspondent.

While I buttoned up my shirt she fixed those dark eyes in mine.

"But you'll always be my first love," she told me. "Always."

"Who me? How can that be? You did it with Chase first."

This reply, I realized later, was wildly inappropriate.

"Chase?"

"Sure. At the roadside park that first night."

"What are you talking about?"

"Well, isn't he, technically, your first love?"

"Only my first lay," she corrected me. "Besides, Chase will always have three or four girls wherever he goes. And, believe me, he won't go far. But you will. You're different."

"How's that?" I asked, and I really wanted to know.

"Because you're sensitive. The most sensitive boy I've ever known."

"Sensitive?" It was a word I wasn't sure of, but certainly more in fashion in those days than now.

"Kipper, you're on a completely different wavelength from all the rest of us, don't you know that?"

I didn't know it, yet I quickly wanted to believe it. I only knew that my name was Kipper Jones, and that until this moment I had been a shortstop, a true pal, a good son, a movie addict, a sex machine, and a part-time delivery boy for my father's store.

"You're capable of real love, Kipper, don't you even know that? And I need love, as it turns out. A true heart, I mean, and, god, we have another whole year of high school before we can get out of here. And if we don't take love where we find it, well, god, I think I'd just break in half."

Mesmerized by Tibby's husky voice and the strangeness of her words, I just looked at her. Clearly, she was the most beautiful naked object in the world. How could I want more? Yet I wanted to speak about the eight of us, the rules, the magic of the last three months.

Then she addressed all that.

"The eight of us won't last the summer," she predicted.

I made some slight gesture with my hand as if I knew that, too, but I didn't.

"There are a lot of little signs, Kipper. I mean, Brad smells a lot like manure these days and a lot of us aren't happy with him.

And Dana, well, she's fragile. She might go goofy on us. And Chase is already looking around. I think he wants to bang every female in the high school including Miss Reinhardt in gym class."

Who among us, I wanted to reply, doesn't?

"Don't get dressed," she said, sighing. "C'mere." She pulled me close and opened herself to me again. "Besides, I don't want to share you with anybody. And now we can do it all the time. Twice a day all summer. Think about it. Three times a day, if that's what you want, then every day during the next school year."

She made a strong argument for love.

"Also, we can talk. I mean, you really listen to me, but you also have lots to say, that's why you're special. And maybe we can actually sleep together. God, I'd love to sleep with you all night. Let me think about it. I'll plan something. Wait, that hurts. Hold it. Now, that's better."

As she talked on, I managed once again to turn myself into molten lava.

We drove back from the Blanco River as a couple.

When I saw Chase back at the store I worried he suspected. That night in the game against Wimberly I made my first two errors of the season, booting one easy grounder that I took on the chin. Distractions. The whole team became sullen after the loss and I felt guilty. Still, Chase didn't say anything.

To my amazement we went back to the hillside that next Friday night, having told her parents we were driving up to Round Rock for the opening of a new cinema complex where a Jack Nicholson movie was showing. The whole evening I kept watching Tibby for a signal, expecting her to make an announcement, but she seemed equally wild for all of us, even Brad. Then, afterward, we all talked music: Tower of Power, Lynard Skynard, ZZ Top, Stevie Wonder, Aerosmith, Cat Stevens, and all the others. Everybody had a different favorite, so minor arguments broke out, then at last I was alone with Tibby in the front seat of the Dodge while Tim and Dana rutted away in the back seat with their usual noises.

"What's going on?" I whispered to Tib. "What were we talking about there at the river? You said you didn't want to share me."

"Ssh, not now," she replied. "Let's just do it."

While we made out the title of an album kept buzzing in my head, a Doobie Brothers title: "What Once Were Vices Are

Now Habits." Was there a song by that title, too? The moon rose over the horizon, giving us its lunatic light. Later on I stretched out on top of the Chevy, confused, and nobody even bothered to say anything to me. The music inside me was definitely funk.

In the days that followed I suspected that Tibby might be giving all the guys special treatment on the side. A clever girl and not an impossible thought. I also decided that Tibby, not my friend Chase, had caused all this to happen, and that what occurred that first night in the roadside park she had definitely orchestrated. She was the one who drove Chase crazy, the one who took off her clothes first, and maybe now, I decided, she manipulated all of us.

Then she phoned to explain.

"Joanna's parents are making her go with them to the Grand Canyon for a whole month. A big summer camping trip. Can you believe it? So that'll break up the group, but also Chase is going to be on the All-Star team which means he'll go away for that. What do you call it?"

"The regional playoffs," I answered sadly, wishing that I was better than a .256 hitter with a good glove and that I'd made the touring all-star team.

"So why should we take the blame for breaking things up? It's happening anyway. That's what I needed to tell you, but couldn't."

"I thought you were just jacking my emotions around," I complained.

"I meant what I said about this summer. Three times a day if you want me to, Kip. We can go back to our spot by the river. Or maybe I can get the key to my dad's deer lease. There's a little cabin on the property. By the time everybody gets back at the end of the summer we'll be together. Just the two of us. It'll just be a thing that happened."

"You seemed to enjoy yourself the other night," I accused her.

"I tried to be a good sport," she countered. "Don't be jealous. Oh, god, Kip, I can't wait to get you alone, I really can't."

When I finally got off the phone I passed my mother in the hallway. She might have been listening in, and asked me who I was talking to.

"Tibby," I said with a sigh. "Maybe we're in love."

Tibby's predictions came true. Chase played on the All-Star

Regional team that finally played a big game in Houston. Joanna, crying and begging to be let off, went with her parents. "The goddamned Grand Canyon," she wailed. "Isn't there a movie about it? Can't they just rent a video?"

We had a last Saturday night together. It was the night I sort of fell for Sylvie. In the back seat of the Dodge she held me close, breathing in my ear, and said quietly, "Kipper, you're the best. Not like anybody else. Gentle and—" Sensitive, I almost said to help her out. She began to cry.

"It's out there, so huge," she whimpered, growing small in my arms. "Life. It's going to gobble us up, isn't it?"

Sylvie was pure feeling. Years later she would be a dancer, dazzling, and that night I kissed her slender neck, watching the tears edge down her cheeks in graceful rivulets. She was soft in a way, I knew, that Tibby would never be.

That night a sadness befell us, a sexual melancholy—although none of us were capable of naming it. We spread out blankets and piled on, all eight of us, our bodies moving over each other slowly, an adagio of touching. Maybe only Tibby and I knew it was goodbye, that idyll, that last long kiss of summer, and we didn't tell what we knew, just as none of us would ever tell others in that little town or strangers who couldn't understand out there in that huge world of which Sylvie spoke.

As I grew older and read some of the books that awaited me, I learned of naked children in the far islands who embraced their sexual lives far sooner than we did—short happy interludes of abandon before the little girls became pregnant and the brief cycles of romance ended. It was true in many places—out on the frozen tundra of the Arctic Circle and in the deepest thickets of Africa—children thrusting themselves into nature where lust, unchecked, becomes curiously innocent. If the eight of us were out of step with the normalcies of a small Texas town, the larger questions remain: what is right, what is natural, what is true and who speaks with authority about any of it?

The ironies overtook us. I became the writer, not Tibby. She became a Dallas lawyer, married with three children. Brad and Dana were once engaged, then quickly married others. Everybody finally married except for Chase, who kicked around the minor leagues for a few years, then joined the Marines and was killed in a skirmish we now call Desert Storm. Friendly fire brought him down.

A dozen years after we left high school I took Sylvie out to dinner in San Francisco. She was the lead dancer in a West Coast ballet troupe, and I was on a political assignment for my magazine when I saw her photo in a newspaper and managed to get a phone number at the theater.

We sat in an open restaurant on a wharf, the place that serves such good abalone, and we began to talk about everybody. She asked about Chase.

"You didn't hear?"

She read my face and tears pooled in her eyes. I told her the few facts I knew.

"Oh, Kipper," she said softly, and she looked out over the bay. No one had called me that in years.

We sat holding hands after the meal. I was newly married and she was engaged, and we ached for one another.

"Was it terrible, what we did?" she asked me.

"No, I believe it was good for all of us," I answered truthfully, though perhaps she didn't quite believe it.

"We were so young," she said, managing a smile. "Sometimes I think nobody was ever that young."

Still holding hands we strolled the wharf while the gulls circled and cried above us. It occurred to me once more that I might have missed Sylvie, missed the great love of my life, but sex, after all, is a mystery; we can possibly be honest about everything except sex, we can know ourselves and not understand it, we can be completely worldly, yet innocent in its wake and impulse.

Sylvie was beautiful and elegant as we walked in silence and I was proud to be at her side. I brought her fingers to my lips and kissed them. In our thoughts, I know, we were in a long ago time, in that strange American twilight before so many of the brutal vulgarities, hidden on a hillside, moving from the old Dodge to the old Chevy, back and forth in a burning game that somehow never burned us out, eight of us, four couples, our sixteen-year-old bodies aglow, far away.

Dove Season

The old man hassled his son all morning, complaining that the coffee wasn't strong enough, that one of the shotguns had been removed from its case too early so that morning dew settled on it, and that the kid's grades—he had finished a year at the local college—had better improve.

"Once mediocre, always mediocre," the old man snapped at him, and his son grew sullen as they started walking the path at the edge of the farm. The old man, Cobb Yoder, was now almost seventy years old. He had driven off his two older sons, so now only Jackdog, nineteen years old and the son of Cobb's second wife, was left to hunt with him.

"Try to get through the day," the old man went on. "Don't step on no rattlesnakes and don't be makin' any fancy swing shots so I get in the line of fire."

"Don't worry, I won't shoot you," Jackdog answered.

"What's that?"

"Nothing. Mind the culvert."

They went into a culvert, then climbed out, going along that edge of the farm that fronted the gray waters of Baffin Bay.

"And slow down, dammit," the old man protested.

By this time Jackdog seethed with anger, but kept silent.

They went another hundred yards, stepping over an old coil of barbed wire and crossing a patch of weeds, but no birds flew up.

"I bet you miss football season," Cobb said, making a first feeble attempt at real conversation.

"Not a bit," Jackdog answered, and he knew well enough why his father mentioned it. After all, it was only six-man football played on a dusty field up at the Riviera Beach school, but it gave the old man an opportunity, after years of having no sons to watch at the local games, to sit in the stands and brag with his drinking buddies. For a minute Jackdog remembered the games, the girls, and the Garza boys and other pals on the team, but he didn't miss any of it.

"You just won't say, but you liked football," the old man persisted.

"No, because when I played linebacker I never hit hard enough to suit you and when I played fullback I never ran far enough," Jackdog told him. "So I don't miss it one damn bit."

That ended that.

The complaints started again when Cobb said, "I notice you didn't shake out your boots this morning. You could've stuck your foot right down on a scorpion." Jackdog kept on walking.

When the sun came up they opened the thermos and drank coffee Jackdog had made, eating a wedge of cheese with it.

"Where in hell are the birds?" the old man asked the sky.

Jackdog knew how to keep quiet and irritate his father, so he did.

After finishing his coffee Cobb said, "Okay, we turn inland. We'll hunt them two long fence rows, c'mon."

"I'll stay along the beach," Jackdog replied.

"What for? Ain't no birds here."

"I'll take my chances."

"If you didn't wanta hunt with me today, you should've said so."

Cobb could hunt alone, Jackdog told himself, and once again he let the silence stand between them until finally he added, "Meet you back at the shack at lunch time. We'll see who found some birds and who didn't."

"All right then," his father said with an angry snort, and he thrust the empty thermos back into Jackdog's hands and stalked off.

Walking along, Jackdog's anger ebbed away. The midday heat of September hadn't yet started and he enjoyed shaking out his aching limbs, having slept in a bedroll in the yard outside the shack where, once, long ago, his grandfather had lived out his last days. Exiled to the far end of the Yoder farm, his grandfather: a three room shack, useless now, with a rickety dock that stuck out sixty feet into the waters of the bay. He never really knew old Jack Yoder, but his mother told him stories: a leathery old man, alone, playing solitaire, fishing for drum and other less than edible fish, coming up to the big house on Sundays for supper.

A dove flew up, but far out of range.

Loyola Beach lay to the east of Baffin Bay, a salty shallows between Padre Island and the South Texas mainland. Every springtime rattlesnakes floated across these briny waters, coming ashore at Loyola to occupy a thorny countryside of mesquite trees, nettles, cactus, yucca, lizards, and scorpions. Along the beach sad driftwood and the rotten carcasses of fish gathered in a residue of oil, smelly seaweed, bottlecaps, defecation, and slime. Where the road ended at the boat ramp the ramshackle Fisherman's Inn stood perched on pilings, serving everything fried: shrimp, filets, potatoes, oysters, hush puppies and Mexican beans. At the weathered dock a few misguided fishermen sometimes pulled their faded boats up to the rusted pumps. The old man loved the Inn and all his beer drinking buddies inside it, all of them content to gather in a place as grim as the landscape itself.

Just north of the Inn the Yoder land started: more than a thousand acres hacked out of a prickly terrain by Grandfather Jack, his son Cobb, and Cobb's sons, then given over to cotton farming. When the earth was turned over for the fall planting thousands of doves arrived and for a few days the Yoders and their farm workers, especially the large Garza family, enjoyed the shooting.

Two birds, flushed out as Cobb went along the fence row, flew with the strong southern breeze so that Jackdog, giving them a big lead, brought them down. Two good quick shots. He started across the soft field to pick them up.

"Dogs! We need ourselves some dogs!" he said aloud as he made his way over the furrows. That was another thing to be angry about: having not a single dog. They had Beau and Spirit, once, but Cobb neglected them and when they finally died the old man offered the opinion that a man who was a good wing shot didn't really need a retriever in the month of September when the ground lay so bare.

Jackdog circled the field, found the birds and placed them in his pouch. After walking back to the path beside the beach, lifting his boots high over the furrows, he was sweaty and pissed off again.

The sorry, mean-spirited, stingy, stubborn, dumb son of a bitch: he had recently raised a hand against Jackdog's mother again after all the promises that it wouldn't happen another time. The argument: a pair of shoes she had bought for him, a pair he claimed he didn't need. In spite of himself, Jackdog went down a list. No dogs. Farm equipment in lousy shape. The Garzas constantly and rightfully angry, so that Tony finally quit in disgust, went off, and joined the army. Beer and bullshit every night at the Inn. Something had to be done.

Suddenly the birds came up.

They came from the fence rows by the dozens, sailing on the rising breeze, heading from his left to right so fast that he could only shoot, load, and shoot again. From downwind they came and kept coming in a long rope of frantic wings. Swinging his gun, giving them a big lead, he pulled off shot after shot, at war with the whole dove population of South Texas, it seemed, missing dozens while stopping to re-load. One, two, a double: he never missed. The old Stevens felt wonderful as it warmed in his hands. He himself felt oiled and ready as if he had waited all his hunting years—since he was nine years old—for this moment.

Once, stopping to load again, he listened for the sound of Cobb's gun, but heard nothing.

As they kept coming he stood on the beach path firing toward the field, dropping birds for perhaps thirty minutes until his ammo started running out. The morning sun glared at him, but he glared back and, once, he made an impossibly long shot on a bird so far away that he knew he'd never go look for it. It went down on the horizon like a stone.

He killed birds until he felt like a man who possessed the day, himself, and pure nature. A deep exhilaration boiled up inside him and he knew it was the greatest feat of shooting he had ever heard about, a hunter's dream, and a story he would later tell.

And still the birds came on, dark flights of them, coming in clusters and very fast. He kept firing until his ammo was gone, and with his last shot he got a double, feeling heroic and blessed.

When his shotgun was hot and empty he let out a yelp of raw pleasure.

As he trudged into the field once again to pick them up, he heard for the first time the report of Cobb's gun somewhere to the east: a single, rather forlorn little bump of sound.

He picked up forty-three birds.

On the long walk back toward the shack the pouch became a steaming burden, but his thoughts were pleasantly addled at what he had done. He didn't mind the weight. As his eyes drifted over the gray waters of Baffin Bay even that pitiful sight looked curiously beautiful in the September sun.

At the shack he cleaned the birds the way Cobb taught him: pushing out the breast of each bird with the pressure of his two thumbs, then tossing the bloody carcasses away. Jackdog remembered seeing old man Garza doing this with one hand: his thumb squeezing a dove's breast up and out. It was generally agreed that a dove's legs and thighs weren't worth anybody's trouble.

Jackdog tossed the remains of the dead birds down a dusty slope onto the beach: feathers, gore, all of it in a messy pile for the scavengers to clean up. Afterward he washed at the tap beside the rickety porch of the shack, then started a campfire with twigs and driftwood.

Cooking up the birds: the last of a tradition. In the old days the Garzas and other workers joined the Yoders in an evening picnic on the first day of dove season. The men cooked for the women. Today was a pale reminder of those times: a single skillet now, a midday lunch, no dogs, no older brothers, no women, no Garzas, just the old man and himself. Resenting it, Jackdog peeled two potatoes and opened a can of salsa, then went to the truck, removed the cooler, and opened a beer. Gliding over the waters of the bay two gulls called to each other.

He thought about his mother. She kept all of Cobb's books, doing all the complex accounting, and in recent years had even started making the deals with the cotton gin. A slender woman, shrewd and tender, she left Cobb to his nights at the Inn and to his days running around the countryside in his pickup. His sexual demands were long over, but his gruff complaints still bore down on her, so she earned what she had from the marriage. Jackdog remembered how she sat in the stands two years ago when he still played football: her hands over her mouth, her eyes worried.

Cobb appeared, coming toward the beach through the furrows.

"Just got two damned birds," the old man announced, glancing at the sizzling skillet. "You get some?"

"A few," Jackdog admitted, and he nodded toward that steep pathway to the beach littered with feathers, blood, and scrawny necks and wings. Cobb shuffled over for an indifferent look.

"I betcha didn't put all the breasts in plastic sacks," he managed.

"They're in the cooler warmin' up your beer."

"And what're you cookin' for?"

"Lunch," Jackdog replied, biting off the word. In spite of himself, his anger flared up again.

"Well, it's too hot for a big meal," Cobb said, and he wiped down his shotgun and placed it in its leather case. "Hear what I'm sayin'? It's too hot to eat."

"Want me to clean your two birds?"

"Why, hell no," Cobb answered him, and he tossed both birds down the pathway toward the others. "I'm takin' the truck back to the house, so I reckon you can eat by yourself, if that's what you want, then walk back."

That did it for Jackdog. He rose from tending the fire, then kicked hard, sending the skillet flying. Hot grease and dove meat scattered around the yard.

"Now that is one asshole thing to do," Cobb told him, but before he could say anything else Jackdog pounced on him, turned him, lifted him by the scruff of his hair and the seat of his pants, and hurled him into that gory mess of dead birds. Cobb didn't stop rolling until he hit the beach, but he bounced up quickly, muddy, a smear of blood—not his own—on his reddening cheek.

"You ungrateful little bastard," Cobb spat out as he started back the same way, his boots sliding over the wet feathers of the dead birds.

"Come on up," Jackdog said evenly. "Raise a hand to me like you did to Mama and I'll break it off for you. Complain one more damn time and I'll close your mouth. You've had your run."

Cobb clawed his way back into the yard, but was short of breath. While he sputtered and gathered himself together, Jackdog had hold of him again. This time he sent the old man flying backward down the same slope.

"I ought to make you live out here in the same shack where you put grandfather," Jackdog told him. "But I don't want to see that much of you. You can move into one of them smelly rooms above the Inn. Better yet, move your ass into Kingsville. Into some damn condo. Come out for Sunday dinner if you want to, but tell me when you're comin' so I'll be gone."

He spoke smoothly, everything natural and impromptu, fluid, like the shooting of so many dove in the morning sunlight.

Cobb flailed around on his back down in the slime.

"And don't try to money whip us 'cause mama knows what's in the books—all the shit you've tried over the years—and I'd just as soon send your sorry ass to jail. You don't know the IRS from a bottle of Shiner. You don't even know cotton farming these days and that's why I'm takin' it over! Because I still know how to work and I'm sober enough to keep the damn farm in the black!"

Cobb made his way through all the little corpses again, wheezing, his face swollen with anger. He had a muddy stone in his fist and meant to use it.

"You've never had a friend or worker you've managed to keep," Jackdog went on. "If I can get Tony Garza out of the army and back here, we'll show you some goddamned cotton farming. Treat your workers right and they'll show you a profit, you dumb, sorry, tight-fisted old fart!"

Cobb cocked his arm with the muddy stone and stumbled forward, but Jackdog had him again. He used Cobb's weight against him, dodging the feeble swipe, then caught him in the crotch, lifted him fully off his feet, and hurled him over the side of the embankment for the third time. At the bottom, covered with sticky feathers, his white hair rumpled, Cobb lay back to rest for a spell.

"You can't even go up the right fence row," Jackdog said evenly, standing at the edge of the yard and peering down at him. "You chased off two sons who worked themselves to death for you. One of 'em's ten times brighter than you are and what's he? A tractor salesman! And what're you? A big-assed braggart who wore out the first Mrs. Yoder like you wore out the dogs! And my own mama, too, except she's too gentle to tell you so, but I will! You sorry ass! Get up here so I can throw you back down where you belong!"

"I'm real partial to dove and you ruined 'em," Cobb managed.

"Don't talk to me about dove! I shoot half the birds in Kleberg County and what do you do? Lay around on the beach!"

"I didn't elect to come down here," Cobb quickly added.

"If I ever let your miserable face back in the house, keep it locked away in your room!" Jackdog told him, and in spite of the tone the old man heard some small possibility.

"Well, sure, your mama don't want me sleepin' in her room. Where else do I stay put except my own damn room?"

"You should apologize to her every day for the rest of your sorry life! And get down on your knees and apologize to both my half brothers! And ask the Garzas to forgive you for all the shit you dumped on them! I'm deeding them land we've cleared and some we haven't because, by god, they've earned it. And before you die you can kiss my ass!"

Cobb sighed heavily and struggled to his feet once more. "Now here I come, so don't keep yourself so riled up. You could hurt a man carryin' on with such a terrible temper as I see you've got."

"Whenever you step outta line I intend to whip you like a dog," Jackdog informed him. "And you're outta line anytime I say."

Cobb clawed his way up the incline once again, then stood before Jackdog winded and flushed. In time he picked up the half cooked breast of a dove, brushed it off, and seemed content to keep it as a souvenir.

"How about a beer?" he asked, trying to concoct a grin.

"Why don't you walk down to the Inn and get your own," Jackdog told him. "I worked all night icing down the cooler, packed gear, laid out food and ammo, then started lunch, but you didn't appreciate any of it. Take care of you own damned requirements. Later, if you're too drunk to walk home from the Inn, phone home. Mama might have mercy on your lazy ass, but not me."

"Now give a man one beer," Cobb argued, as if this much might be salvaged from the day.

But Jackdog gathered up the camp items, even the hot skillet and tossed them into the rear of the pickup with a loud clang. Cobb followed him around during all this, pleading his case for just one single bottle of beer, just one bottle to see him off on his trip down the beach to the Inn.

"Ask me one more time and I'm stuffin' you down the bird slot again," Jackdog finally snapped at him. With that he jumped into the truck, started the engine and drove away. When he glanced in the rearview mirror he saw Cobb—his mouth tight and sealed—as he turned his footsteps toward the Inn.

By the time he drove the mile back to the house Jackdog's thoughts had returned to shooting dove: a great day, a glorious series of wing shots, impossible shots, five birds with two barrels, a closing double, and he felt his jurisdiction over the fields, the distant waters of the bay, and the creatures of the air.

Money Whipped

Knox liked movies and decided to make one.

Why not? Since selling his business—the manufacture of steel cable—he had lots of cash. Apart from that he had only his cranky mother, his new wife Beezie, two houses, three cars, and a plane he hadn't learned to fly.

He thought up a good movie story—Beezie helped on it—then went about finding a screenwriter. He knew exactly what he wanted: another Texan, male, bookish but not some wimp, a guy who at least played golf, and somebody with real screen credits, not some pretender or run-of-the-mill suck up.

It took him awhile to learn about The Writer's Guild, then more time to pick names from their membership list: Texans, male, screen credits. All this began in April, but in the heat of July arrangements were finally made. A writer named Drew Gamble agreed to fly to Houston for an interview. They met in Knox's big apartment on Riverway for cocktails, planning for dinner later at Café Annie except they drank too much and never got there.

Beezie wore a glittering blouse open to her navel, a pair of white shorts, and tennis shoes that she kicked underneath the glass coffee table. She crossed her long legs and pumped her lacquered toes ever so slightly, keeping a sensual beat to a music perhaps only she heard.

Drew, the writer, currently lived in London and possessed a great mane of blond hair. He dressed in tight faded jeans, a gleaming white T-shirt, and an unlined and wrinkled summer sports jacket, blue, that matched his eyes. Perhaps forty, he moved and looked like a younger man because of the hair—coiffed to look wild and unruly—and struck an attitude that suggested both danger and insouciance. He looked as though he had just flown in from a war.

Knox, paunchy and darkly tanned, enthusiastic as always, showed Drew the view from the terrace with the Houston skyline spread out before them, and tried to make small talk while aching to tell his writer the plot points of their story. Beezie gazed over the rim of her glass, wearing it like a mask that hid half her face, her large brown eyes never blinking.

When they settled in the sitting room Knox began walking and gesturing with his tumbler of bourbon. "See, Drew, the Vietnamese came to Texas after the war. Refugees. They were the friendlies, of course, who had worked with our guys in Saigon. Anyway, they settled on the coast and started shrimp fishing. But the established fishermen down there resented them, so there were, like, acts of violence. Guys burning boats. A feud. One refugee got killed. All this was in the newspapers. So in our story there's this lonely vet. He was wounded in Vietnam and had some Vietnamese pals. Maybe one of them saved his life. So when the shrimp war gets nasty he throws in with the refugees. Maybe there's a love interest. Maybe an American girl, but you decide about that. By the way, you didn't happen to serve in Vietnam, did you?"

"He was too young," said Beezie from behind her glass.

Drew nodded in response.

"So that's the story," Knox said proudly. "We've got more details, naturally, in the written outline."

"Sounds intriguing," said Drew.

"Also, it's got good movie visuals," Knox continued, filling his glass. "Explosions and boats on fire, all that. And maybe there's an old wise man, a refugee with a white beard, and he and this vet become pals. And the American girl is a lot like Beezie."

"You an actress?" Drew asked.

"I was a model once," she answered. "A long time ago."

They knocked back another drink. Drew soon learned that Beezie was Knox's third wife—they had married six months ago—and that most of the ideas for the movie were hers. Then Knox talked about his former business, steel cable. Aircraft companies used miles of cable in every fuselage and wing, Knox explained, and the shipping companies were also big time buyers. He had warehouses for his cable on every continent, he told Drew, and his real estate purchases had also gone very well.

"Tell him how much you sold for," Beezie urged him.

"Nah, what's the difference? Money is only defined by what you do with it. I like to help my employees and I'm not the kind of guy who ever money whips anybody. And some money needs to be play money, so that's where you and the movie come in. Oh, yeah, did I tell you I watched that African movie you wrote?"

"We rented the video," Beezie added.

"You've got the knack, see, Drew, for exotic settings and people, so I figure you'll do great with the refugees. Also, I checked your price and my sources tell me a writer should always get a boost from his last assignment, so how about my offer?"

"I flew to Houston because I appreciated your offer," Drew said, rattling the ice cubes in his glass. "And I accept. Where do we go from here?"

"Lordy, this is great," Knox said, and he touched Beezie's shoulder as he crossed to the bar. "I'm gonna fill up the glasses!"

"I thought I might head down to the coast for a few days," Drew ventured. "See the actual fishing fleet and talk with a few of the fishermen."

"Get right to work, eh? Great, I like it."

They drank to the movie forming in their heads, to themselves, and to the night that hovered above the city. Then they told one another about their lives, weaving omissions and lies in a pleasant inebriation. Beezie hailed from Kingsville and her good looks, she admitted, had launched her out of South Texas into a world of men with cameras. Her name was Barbara Catherine, BC, Beezie, and as she talked Knox revealed that she was thirty-two years old and that he had a daughter who was thirty-nine. Knox grew up in Dallas, he said, in a place called La Reunion, a prefab housing development on the wrong side of the Fort Worth highway, a shantytown where his father came back from World War II and drank himself into oblivion. Knox outlined his climb to success: odd jobs, factory work, a series of cockeyed inventions that failed to get patents, then the little cable company that he bought in bankruptcy. He had borrowed money to make the down payment, then modified the machines, tooling out a process that made better cable faster.

"Tell you something, Drew," Knox went on. "For just a sport shandy—"

He stopped as Beezie gave him a look.

"For just a short span," he corrected himself, "we live on this earth. Life's precious, then it's over."

From this declaration they began to talk about what each of them believed in. Drew said he believed in the English language, beautiful women, wine with dinner, neatly trimmed fairways, and constant travel. Beezie said people, she really liked all sorts of people, she was a people person. Reciting this, smiling, not unlike the beauty pageant contestant she once was, Beezie watched Knox raise a toast in her direction.

Knox then went into a long ramble about religion. He didn't exactly believe in God, he told them, and predicted that all religion would one day be absorbed into the study of astronomy. The galaxies, he offered, will one day be seen as the miracles they are. From this he began to discuss molecular biology, clones, and the speed of light. Beezie noted that Knox hated organized religion, but was actually a very spiritual person.

Long after midnight they helped Knox to bed. He went from his bourbon haze to a deep sleep, dreaming of the empty spaces between the stars.

Later, his own snoring woke him up. After relieving himself in the bathroom he circled through the apartment. Beezie wasn't in her bed or anyplace else. The French clock tolled four times.

The terrace was empty, too, and he thought, all right, Beezie has driven our writer back to his hotel. Knox slumped in a lounge chair, fighting the suspicion that his young wife and the handsome writer had found each other too appealing. He considered driving over to the Omni and checking the hotel room, but padded through the rooms, turning on the TV then turning it off again, and finally going back to bed. Lying there awake, he heard Beezie returning after five in the morning, then listened while she took a long shower and went to her bed.

Before noon Knox was reading the newspapers and having coffee when Beezie appeared on the terrace. Before he could ask any questions she smiled and said, "God, I stayed up late! I drove Drew back to the hotel, then we sat in the car talking."

"About what?" he asked as casually as possible.

"The script. And I'm not sure if the Vietnamese refugees should, like, be in the movie. I love the idea of a lonely war veteran. He should live in a lighthouse. And this beautiful woman befriends him and, well, maybe it could be a great romantic story."

"No Vietnamese fishermen?"

"Maybe, but really a love story. But we don't have to decide right now. Drew's renting a car and driving down to the coast today. He's probably already gone. He wants to check things out before we make, like, final decisions."

Knox felt grateful that Drew had left town.

He watched Beezie spread jam on a honey bun, then wolf it down. She ate like an animal, filling her cheeks with huge bites so that her cheeks puffed out. She was still a brightness that filled him up and even if his mother didn't like her, he told himself, I do, I could forgive her anything, I adore her.

Knox's mother, Avis, lived in an old River Oaks mansion that now resembled a Mexican piñata: colored tiles set in crazy patterns on its stucco exterior, a lumpy figurine on the front lawn adorned with shards of colored glass and tile, a rooftop wearing the reindeer from last Christmas, assorted urns around the gardens, a stone sombrero filled with red hibiscus, and mismatched lawn furniture stacked up like a jungle gym alongside the driveway. Beyond a giant mimosa and within sight of those passing in the neighborhood—an otherwise elegant district of sedate homes— stood the cornfield. Avis, now eighty years old and unable to do strenuous gardening, still rolled out her own fresh tortillas and spent her days cooking and eating. She liked red hot jalapeños and popped them down like lemon drops while listening to the old tunes of the Tijuana Brass on her boom box CD player. Over the kitchen stove hung a framed and autographed photo of Cary Grant. Since Knox's first successful days in the cable business Avis had enjoyed her widowhood in this house, a great box of nineteen rooms resided over by a dozen cats who fed on leftover enchiladas. Her son's daily visits—usually for lunch—comprised her social life.

"My prodigy!" she always greeted him, and except for his marriage to Beezie she regarded him as a genius.

At lunch that day, watching him nibble around the edges of a taco salad, Avis asked what was wrong. Nothing, he told her, and they poked at their meal in silence.

"Something's got your appetite," she prodded him, and unable to resist he blurted out the whole story of the previous evening. This prompted her usual litany: Beezie talks like a waitress, she reads with her fingers tracing the words, she has silicone breasts, she can't enter this house, she's just after your money.

He offered all his standard justifications including Beezie's enthusiasms for the act of love, but Avis waved it all away.

"Wanta know what'll happen next?" she asked. "Beezie will concoct a trip for herself. Simple and natural sounding. Like she'll decide to visit her mother—who, by the way, hates her even more than I do. Anyway, she'll leave town and hook up with that writer. You say he wears a wig?"

"Yeah, it's gotta be a wig," Knox said, moaning.

"How old is this screenwriter?"

"Twenty years younger than I am. You think I should hire a private detective to watch him?"

"No, you'll just go crazy knowing more than you do already," Avis told him, biting into her taco.

Knox leaned on his elbow beside his plate of food. "You really think she'll manufacture a trip for herself?"

"Son, if I know you, you'll help her pack, then kiss her goodbye," said Avis.

The lunch before him looked awful, like swill with salsa.

"I'm thinking of flying up to Dallas to see my mother," Beezie informed him that evening as she painted her toenails. She occupied the middle of her giant oval bed, cotton balls wedged between each toe as she applied a coat of golden lacquer.

"You and your mother don't even speak."

"On the phone, no, because she hangs up on me," Beezie countered. "So I need to see her face to face. We need to make up. Maybe I'll take her a nice present."

"Okay, I'll go with you," Knox suggested.

"No, this is a girl thing."

"Then I'll have our pilot fly you into Love Field, so you'll be right there at her place in Highland Park."

"I was thinking of flying commercial."

"You'd rather go through two airports with all your baggage rather than fly into a private terminal?"

Beezie tried a weak smile in response.

"Tell you what," Knox said. "While you visit your mama I'll zip down to the coast and see our writer. Scout some locations with him."

At this suggestion Beezie managed only a defeated nod.

The next morning their pilot flew Beezie up to Dallas, then returned to pick up Knox and to deliver him to a sad little airport on the north side of Nueces Bay. In the meantime Knox phoned Drew, so the writer could meet him with a rented Cadillac. They drove over to Corpus Christi for dinner, talking golf, Texas food, and the movie. In Corpus they found a seafood restaurant adorned with a mural of Venus rising from the sea, then searched the menu for something that wasn't fried.

"Yesterday I ate lunch in this café over in Aransas Pass," Drew said. "Afterward I asked the waitress if they had any Rolaids or Tums. She told me, 'Honey, hell, we make our profit on Rolaids.'"

At that, they had their first real laugh together and started talking in earnest about their movie.

"The Vietnamese fishermen stay in the movie," Knox asserted.

"Sure, who says otherwise? That's what'll give the film all its depth," Drew quickly agreed.

After this Knox doubted that much had passed between Beezie and the writer—who seemed supremely professional. Yet he phoned Beezie that evening, making sure that she stayed at her mother's house in Dallas. Satisfied, then, he phoned his mother who said, no, please she didn't want to talk about her daughter-in-law, no thanks, because she couldn't form a simple declarative sentence about Beezie without using the word *slut*.

The next morning Knox and Drew toured Port Aransas, definitely no tourist spot. They saw rusted out fishing boats, smelly nets piled on outworn docks, old men with leathery faces, scores of aggressive gulls, vacant lots littered with beer bottles and discarded bathroom fixtures, a creaking old ferry, and finally a squat little lighthouse—unoccupied and boarded up.

"We'll go down to city hall and find out who owns this wreck," Knox remarked, walking around it and rubbing his hands together. "We'll buy it or lease it, then refurbish it for the movie. Our wounded war veteran will live here."

Drew gave him an odd smile.

"What?" Knox asked.

"Nothing personal, but I'll always be interested in how money talks," the writer said.

"We're gonna spend, Drew, then make money," Knox promised.

They ate lunch in an establishment that was just the frame of a building: patches of screen tacked around, a sagging roof, and everything seemingly held together by neon tubing that spelled out the names of beers. Drew talked about living in London.

"I was always the quiet type. Played tennis. I was sort of formal and reserved—not like the shitkickers at the University. English major, you know. I lived and thought like a Victorian and when I went to Africa for my research on that movie I wanted to be, oh, Graham Greene or some BBC writer composing brittle dialogue for *Masterpiece Theater*. I wanted to lose my Texas drawl. Go up to Lake Windemere and take melancholy strolls on the forest pathways. But, hey, I was always a Texan—one of the nomadic Texans—and I never had enough money to be all that aristocratic. When you phoned I was thinking about giving up my flat and heading back to Blanco County. If we do this movie, though, I'll have enough in the bank to stick in London for another year and see what happens."

In the extreme midday heat they found a little movie house and sat with large tubs of popcorn watching a bad western. Later they drank beer and listed the great movies: *The Godfather*, *Cabaret*, *Casablanca*. At the docks in the late afternoon they watched the fishing boats come in, and Knox paid out a bouquet of hundred dollar bills so they could join the crew of a professional boat for the next day's fishing. The captain, a crusty little guy who looked like he might have been a general for the Cong, told them to show up at four the next morning with their own food and drink. He pocketed Knox's money, promising to split it with his men.

That evening they filled a cooler with beer, bread, and barbeque, then ate dinner in a smoky bar and talked about women: Knox's wives and two divorced daughters, Drew's many girlfriends and his reluctance to get married: the natural disorders of sex and love.

During this Drew apologized for staying out late with Beezie.

"Nothing happened," he added quickly. "We just sat there talking too long, and I didn't know how to break if off since, well, because she's the wife of the boss and she had all these ideas about our movie. Anyway, I know it must've looked indiscreet staying out so late. And I'm sorry if you worried about it."

"Beezie told me all about it," Knox said. "We won't mention it again. Here, look, I need to give you some cash."

"What for?"

"Pay the rental car outta this," Knox instructed him, and he produced a roll of hundred dollar bills, pushing them into Drew's hands without counting them. "You'll have other expenses. Incidentals. I'll pick up our hotel, naturally, and, wait, I don't really think this is enough."

"It's more than enough," Drew assured him, and they arrived at a familiar male covenant: soldiers in a cause, everything sealed with alcohol, sincerity, and cash. They had a nightcap, then went back to their hotel to sleep.

By dawn they were out on the gulf, the engine of their boat coughing up clouds of diesel while their Vietnamese hosts chewed Red Man tobacco and spat long brown streamers into the waves. On the choppy sea in the midst of fumes and brownish saliva both Knox and Drew felt queasy but devoured their barbeque sandwiches and drank a couple of beers each before ten o'clock in the morning. The crew members sipped from Mason jars filled with clear liquid—possibly rice wine, possibly vodka—while working, chewing, and spitting.

By noon, hopelessly seasick, both Knox and Drew heaved at the rails as the boat moved through rising swells. As the crew worked the nets, hauling in shrimp, they were both too sick to watch the effort. They staggered around midship as observers, but saw little because every few minutes they hurried back to the rails.

"Keep out of way!" shouted the little captain, and they nodded grimly as they puked. They knew they were comic and pathetic as they gasped for air in the diesel fumes, then watched in horror as a crew member converted himself into a chef and turned the wheelhouse into a galley where he boiled rice for the midday meal. The electric winch sent up its high whine and the gulls circled overhead with a descant of mocking laughter.

"Why're we here?" Drew asked, trying to grin. His shirt was fouled and his beautiful hair hung down in strings.

That evening Knox spoke with Beezie on the phone. Her mother had thrown her out, so she had checked into a fancy Oak Lawn hotel.

"Lemme come down there with you guys," she pleaded.

"I'll be back in Houston tomorrow and I'll see you there," Knox told her. "I'll send the plane for you around noon."

After the phone call Knox sat thinking how he had met Beezie and how much he loved her. He had occupied a barstool in Anthony's when she appeared at his side to take his order: a little too busty for modeling anymore, sassy, and with eyes that looked as though they had just popped open in surprise. He told her that he owned his own airplane and asked if she wanted to fly to Bimini and she answered, sure, why not, let's go, and where exactly is Bimini? They didn't come back until she sported a five-carat diamond and his last name. After all, his big apartment was hollow and full of echoes. His daughters, he knew, wanted him to die and leave them more than they deserved and he felt his age, over sixty and climbing.

That evening Knox and Drew settled their stomachs with whiskey and soda. They found a roadhouse over toward Rockport with a three-piece western band playing a medley of Patsy Cline songs.

Drew was soon drunk with his arm draped over Knox's shoulders, saying, "Knox, you're the king of cable and what do you do? You decide to make a movie with a serious social message! It makes me proud to know you."

Knox, less drunk, listened and smiled. Such flattery made him uneasy and usually preceded a major hit, so he interrupted Drew's oncoming speech with another roll of hundred dollar bills.

"What I gave you wasn't enough," he said. "Remember I told you that? So here, take this."

As Knox pressed it into Drew's hands the screenwriter's protests were short. Then he leaned close and said, "We're gonna see our names on the big screen, Knox, I feel it. This movie'll happen. But it's also more than that: we're gonna be friends for a long time. You know that, too, doncha?"

Knox was experienced enough to know that some deep candor was about to take place, something confessional, something that money often pried loose. He had seen it dozens of times and never knew exactly what form it would take, yet as he watched Drew slowly pushing the money into the tight pockets of his faded jeans he felt it coming.

"Knox, my friend, remember our first night together? When you went to bed drunk? Beezie went to her room, Knox, and put on this—well, it was a little gown."

"Uh huh," Knox replied, and he topped off their whiskies.

"A gown. Transparent." Drew leaned in, lowering his voice into intimate confidence. "A little gown with flowers on it. So then she drove me back to my hotel. The Omni. You know the little gown I'm talking about?"

Knox felt his chest flutter as if he might have a heart attack, but managed a nod.

"Anyway, Knox, we didn't go directly to the hotel. I want to tell you this because you and I—well, we're friends now. So Beezie and I drove to this little park down by the river, Knox, and this little gown, well, she didn't have any panties on underneath it."

Knox wanted the writer to shut up, but the money and liquor prompted him to go on.

"Knox, I'm only a man. A mortal creature. All my life I've wanted to be a gentleman. A Victorian gentleman. All the courtesies. I do not put heavy moves on women. Never. I didn't put a move on Beezie, not so much as a signal. I also wondered if you two might do this sort of thing with others—friends or strangers or business partners. How could I know? So I was a little drunk myself that evening. And confused."

"Enough details," Knox managed.

"We've come a long way together in a short time, Knox, and I want to feel good about us, man to man. And unless you say otherwise I consider it a one time thing."

"Yeah, let's call it that," Knox agreed.

"Good. Fine. It's over, then, with Beezie and me," Drew said, and he finished his drink, taking a deep satisfied breath. His hair, Knox noted, was finely coiffed again, so that since their time on the gulf the writer must've worked on his hairdo.

Drew started a more jovial topic. "So if we shoot this movie, Knox, I guess you and I won't head out into the gulfstream again, will we? I mean, hell, let the second unit shoot the scenes out there! We've had it with shrimp fishing, right?" The writer laughed louder and longer than necessary.

"You're right about that," Knox replied, trying to smile.

They went to the parking lot and found the Cadillac. A hot and humid evening: a sticky gulf breeze and, far off, a wall of giant thunderheads rising above the horizon with soft displays of lightning.

"Let me have the car keys," Knox said.

"Sure, good idea. You drive."

As Knox accepted the car keys he took a deep breath and said, "Drew, our movie deal is cancelled. You stay here. You're fired and I don't want you in the car on the way back to the hotel."

"Hold on," said Drew. "I was just tryin' to be honest."

"We're not talking anymore. You got cash, so go away."

With this, Knox slipped inside the Cadillac and clicked the locks, shutting Drew out.

"I thought we were friends!" Drew shouted through the closed window. "I wanted to be honest with you! At least give me a ride back to the hotel so we can talk, okay?"

"Be a Victorian gentleman with somebody else's wife," Knox told him, and drove off.

Driving alone through the darkness Knox wished he still owned his business, that he was still spinning out cable. He longed for his company and his old office. I sold out for money, he told himself, and now my daughters love money, not me.

He drove as if following where the headlights led.

Maybe Beezie's the same, he said to himself. She's broken my heart and she's everything, she's what's left of me, and I can't spend the rest of my life in my mother's kitchen.

He picked up the car phone, dialed his pilot, and told him to head for the airport and to prepare to fly. Then he phoned Beezie and, amazingly, she was in her suite and seemed happy to hear from him.

"Get dressed and grab a taxi for Love Field," he said. "I'll be in the air within the hour and I need a kiss."

"Knox, thank goodness! I've been missin' you, Sweetie," she responded, and he wanted to cry for joy. He'd tell her later that Drew didn't work out. He'd say he was sorry, he knew, although for what, exactly, he wasn't sure.

The movie, he decided, was stupid. I know nothing about shrimp fishing, the feud, Vietnam veterans, good writing, the Gulf of Mexico, camera angles, or acting like a producer. Pretentious.

Yet, at seventy miles an hour the night seemed to settle around him and he thought, wait, why not a movie? And no apologies for a young and beautiful new wife. Starting over suits me fine. I'll go talk to my daughters—and not to money whip them, but to ask for their affection if they have an ounce left. And I'll say, Beezie, maybe we didn't go at this the right way, maybe we made mistakes, but who knows if we can make a movie or not? And the next screenwriter will be older than I am. Ancient.

Texas Hold 'Em

When Mackie went for her interview with Ray Bob Brown and his wife, Sheila, she concentrated on keeping her pitch snobbish and simple. She also cautioned herself about laughing out loud—she had a laugh like a horse—and about squirming around as she sometimes did when she was nervous. Mackie was a Texas blonde, a former basketball player and psychology major, pretty enough to use her good looks to advantage, and yet she wanted to land this job by being prepared and clever.

They met for dinner at the Mansion on Turtle Creek, a Dallas establishment with a cuisine that occasionally featured fifty dollar tacos. Overdressed dingers occupied the surrounding tables and the food looked good, but Mackie couldn't eat. She took a deep breath and went right to business.

"You want to enjoy your money and have fun, but you also want to be seen in the right places at the right times," she began. "I mean, you don't want to go places out of season or look cheap or otherwise embarrass yourselves."

Ray Bob took a spoonful of lobster bisque, blinked, and just gawked at her. He didn't wear enough suit to cover his ample belly. Although he had recently sold his business—retiring with enough money to impress all the newspaper columnists in Dallas—his clothes were still Bill Blass or something off the rack and he needed coaching.

"Say you go to Aspen next ski season," Mackie went on. "You take the biggest suite at the Ritz Carlton—which, by the way, was probably booked a year ago. But say you landed it. It would be even more impressive if you stayed at one of the big private homes on the slopes. A place that belongs, say, to an ex-President or a famous movie director. Prestige. You hire the right cook and driver. You throw small parties after the last run."

"Hell, I don't even ski," Ray Bob put in.

"Let the girl talk," Sheila added.

"Personally," Mackie suggested, "I'd go to Saint Moritz. I even know a house for you there, a big one so you could invite guests."

"I do know for a fact there's some damn nice fly fishing streams up around Aspen," Ray Bob said, finishing off a tray of wafers.

"Yes, but New Zealand's the hot spot for fishing," Mackie gently offered. "You'd want to stay in exactly the right lodge on North Island. Fish with the perfect gear. Get your name dropped in fly fishing circles. It's a subtle business. And I'll suggest places to go and serve as a kind of publicist for you."

"Can't you eat your first course, Honey?" Sheila inquired.

"No, I have to get through this," Mackie said, and in spite of herself that croaking laughter came out. "Sorry."

"Hell, Honey, don't be nervous around us," Sheila told her. "That's why we're here tonight. Tryin' to figure out exactly what a recreational counselor does."

Mackie realized that the Browns had ordered a rigid background check on her before agreeing to this interview, but she had also turned up a few facts about them. After high school in Waxahachie, Sheila went to work as a waitress in the coffee shop at the old Adolphus Hotel where she met Ray Bob. He had just started his container business in his father's empty barn out beyond Oak Cliff, and she became his office manager, his wife, then his vice-president before they sold out to International Packagers, retired, and began trying to figure out what all that money meant.

"We want to see the world and raise a little hell," Ray Bob confided. "But we've been working folks and now we need a few suggestions."

"Our friends the Tolberts in Amarillo hired this art buyer," Sheila added. "They told us they were thinking about a recreation counselor, so we decided to get one first."

"We own just the one big old house," Ray Bob mused. "Maybe we should get a couple more. Something by the ocean. Would you buy east coast or west coast?"

"Why not just travel and establish yourselves for a year or so?" Mackie replied thoughtfully. She tapped a blue fingernail on her wine glass, a fingernail that perfectly matched the color of her eyes. "Why not pamper yourselves for awhile? Travel and meet folks? Learn a few power moves. Just relax. Why worry about houses?"

"Now you're talkin'," Sheila said.

"Eat some of this, okay?" Ray Bob urged her. "Look how skinny you are."

"She's not a bit skinny up top," Sheila observed.

They became so relaxed, laughing together, that Mackie began to suspect that she had the job. By the time the main course was finished—Mackie still just picked at her food—the Browns asked if she might consider traveling with them for a few months. At this she gave them another loud guffaw, then stammered, "Sure, I guess, why not?"

"If you traveled with us, maybe we ought to know if you have any personal complications, too," Sheila ventured. "A sick mama. Or a steady boyfriend. You free to just get up and go?"

"The love of my life so far, well, we just recently broke up," Mackie assured them. "I found out he was after this other girl at our health club."

"Men cannot be trusted a lick," Sheila intoned. "Except for Ray Bob. And that's because he's impotent. It finally happened to him."

"Goddammit, Sheila," Ray Bob said.

"Dead as a doornail," Sheila went on. "Me, I'm relieved. For me, it's like time off for good behavior."

"Goddamn," Ray Bob said to the crystal chandelier overhead.

"Do I have the job, then?" Mackie asked, making sure.

"You've already started," Sheila replied. "Hell, Honey, I'd trust anyone with a god awful laugh like yours."

The two women had a good laugh together, then Mackie picked up a *crème brulee* and began spooning in into her wide smile.

"There are some things, Sheila, you just goddamn don't have to tell," said Ray Bob, and he folded his arms, sulking, and pushed away from the table, his appetite gone.

Mackie and the Browns spent September and October that year at Newport, anchored at Bannister's Wharf in a refitted schooner. Its decks were gleaming teakwood and shiny brass.

It attracted so many leering tourists that the Browns tried to rent one of the grand cottages on Ochre Point and finally took rooms at Ivy House. Mackie studied a history of New England society and explained to Ray Bob and Sheila the significance of Hammersmith Farm where Jackie grew up, Henry James, the Astors, the von Bulows, and Doris Duke. Sheila read a biography of Stanford White while Ray Bob drank beer every noon at The Mooring, watching J-boats cruise into the dock. He decided that he needed Texas barbecue, so had ten pounds of it flown in every day, a small, crude excess that made him popular at the bar and resulted in new acquaintances. One of them, a Rhode Island native, known as Mr. TJ, impressed Ray Bob by announcing that he had never actually earned money, just always had it.

"Then what do you do?" Ray Bob asked him.

"Nothing. But I always sleep until noon before starting it."

Later, Mr. TJ confided in Ray Bob that he didn't regard earned money as insignificant. "You must never get the idea that I'll ever hold it against you that you worked for it," he said one afternoon when he was slightly drunk and full of barbecue.

Ray Bob repeated this strange observation to Mackie, asking if Mr. TJ might have been joking.

"No, probably not," she advised him. "He was just talking about old money and new money."

"What the hell is old money?" Ray Bob wanted to know.

"It's a European thing," she explained. "Kind of snotty."

One afternoon when Sheila and Mr. TJ's wife went off to shop in Little Compton, Ray Bob and Mackie were alone on the schooner. She wore a sweatshirt over bikini bottoms, padding around the galley barefoot while making grilled cheese sandwiches.

"Aren't you going over for beers with Mr. TJ?" she asked.

"I should," Ray Bob told her. "Because you're drivin' me crazy and I can't stay around here."

She knew that she should go put on more clothes immediately, but gave him the nervous horse laugh instead and slid her legs out of sight beneath the bar while perching herself on a wicker stool. Their sandwiches sat before them, but Ray Bob just poked his with a stubby finger.

"The other night at that fancy inn," he began, gearing his voice down into a terrible sincerity. "I wanted the orchestra to play something slow so I could dance with you—just hold you!"

"Ray Bob, c'mon, please."

"I'm old and fat and goofy, but I want to be touched. Just a tiny caress. A woman's touch." He came around the bar and stood beside her. "You're so goddamned pretty that it breaks a man's heart," he said, and his drawl ascended into a whine. "And, awright, you know the truth about me: I can't get it up. But my thoughts are the same and I'm on fire. And it's your fault. Tell you what. I'll make you a deal. I'll give you a hundred dollars every time you kiss me. How about it?"

"You old goat," she said, grinning, and trying to shame him out of this with a mocking sarcasm.

"Two hundred, then. What'll it take?"

"Ray Bob, this is harassment. It's a bribe and a threat."

"Two hundred cash. We're talkin' about just one goddamned kiss. A thirty second kiss, say, and if it disgusts you, then you don't ever have to do it again."

"Two hundred? One time only?" She hated that she weakened in this.

"If you say so," he answered, and he sounded forlorn and desperate.

Tiny waves lapped against the schooner: little tremors. Mackie became acutely aware of the bawling seagulls out on the quay.

"Don't touch my breasts if we do this," Mackie instructed him. "Even with your thumbs, so you're holding my rib cage and copping a feel. I hate that. And no tongue."

"Well, goddamn, what do I get?"

"One kiss. Lips slightly parted. No funny business."

In order to prove that his word was good, Ray Bob opened his wallet and started counting out the cash. He came up short.

"Hold on," he said, breathlessly, and he went for more.

Sitting there with her cold cheese sandwich, Mackie felt shameful. Prostituting kisses. Damn. She remembered a night back in high school when she had agreed to let Billy Joe Pitts kiss her and they ended up in the back of his daddy's ancient Ford pickup with the steering wheel tied down and the throttle slightly open. While they rolled around on blankets the old Ford bumped slowly over acres of empty prairie, knocking down an occasional mesquite bush or an ant hill until it came to rest against a barbed wire fence, its slick tires throwing out little wisps of dry dust, its engine knocking in time with their pounding heartbeats. Mackie had to wrestle Billy Joe that night—she was considerably stronger—because such kissing and fondling led to babies, she knew, and to the doldrums of family life, hourly wages, houses in wayward little towns, and the end of dreams. She wanted to see Venice and Paris, instead, and to wrestle away millionaires who adored her—which now, if Ray Bob tried anything too bold, she might actually be doing.

He came back with his stash and counted out the full amount. She scooped up the money, turned out of his line of vision, tucked it into her bikini, then turned back to receive his embrace.

"Now don't go tellin' Sheila about this," he warned her as he stepped forward.

"Watch the hands," Mackie commanded him in return. She was more than four inches taller.

The kiss was neither awful nor pleasant. Ray Bob, after all, was a sweet, paunchy, hopeful, and deeply grateful soul, and with their mouths softly grinding together for half a minute she assumed he was getting his money's worth.

"Damn," he said when they finished. "That's the best thing's happened to me in two years." His eyes stayed closed in rapture.

"Just don't get carried away," Mackie cautioned him as they moved back at arm's length.

"One a day like that," he said, opening his eyes and fixing her with his gaze. "Thirty seconds. Two hundred a kiss. I'm hooked. I've gotta have 'em."

"C'mon, Ray Bob," she drawled, trying to kid him out of it.

"I can afford it. Don't worry. Some folks like cocaine and I like kisses."

She turned, leaned against the bar, and held her head in her hands. You're a recreation counselor, she told herself. As if trying to wake up from amnesia, she repeated her own name. Mackie. You're on a boat far from home in a strange country. Your professional dignity is shot. You love money too much. That's an extra fourteen hundred a week for three and a half minutes of hands-off kissing, Mackie, and you're weak and superficial.

In late October they went to London for shopping. Sheila and Ray Bob insisted on telling strangers and doormen at The Ritz about riding on top of sightseeing busses, pushing through the crowds at the Tower, and watching every changing of the palace guards. Their suite filled up with plastic souvenirs: replicas of Big Ben, Queen Victoria, the Beatles, and Winston Churchill.

For nine days Ray Bob had Mackie trapped in the suite while Sheila explored Harrod's and Lilywhite's.

"That's the last kiss," Mackie finally protested. "I mean it, Ray Bob, just pay my salary, no bonuses. To tell the truth, I'm feeling guilty as hell."

"Okay, no more kisses, anything you say," he agreed, but later he cornered her between the TV console and a rubber plant in the parlor of the suite. She stomped his foot in self-defense, escaped, and later went to Sheila.

"Does he stick his tongue in your mouth?" Sheila wanted to know, her eyes narrowing.

"No, that's not allowed. And he doesn't touch any, well, vital parts. That's not allowed, either."

"You've got rules and he obeys them?"

"Sheila, the extra money screwed up my head and I'm really sorry. I like my job, but I'll understand if you send me back to Texas."

Sheila took a few minutes to think it over. "It's all right with me if you kiss him for a little extra cash," she finally said, sighing. "Lord knows, somethin's making him happy. And he leaves me the hell alone."

"I worry that I'll revive him. What if his hormones make a comeback?"

"In that case, I'll probably know about it, too," Sheila said. "Keep me advised."

That week the Tolberts arrived from Amarillo, checked into several rooms, and became constant companions of the Browns. The Tolberts, Deva and Buck, were small, loud, and heavily tanned as if they had been baked down to muffin size. Accompanying them to London was their art expert and buyer, Don Jacks. They arrived in a rented Bentley, raised a ruckus over a misplaced bag at reception, and later presented themselves at tea when Ray Bob wore his new Savile Row suit.

Don Jacks had grown up poor in Odessa—no oil wells, no land, not a single damn steer, he later said. He was lanky and handsome with the shrewd gaze of a poker player and Buck Tolbert flew him all over the world to buy paintings and sculptures for their collection. Don moved and spoke with unbelievable arrogance so Mackie didn't like him at first, but as the Browns and Tolberts huddled at close range and yelled at one another while taking tea, Don leaned back on a brocade pillow there in the hotel sitting room, grinned, picked a sugared biscuit off a porcelain serving tray, and confessed to Mackie that he didn't know a thing about art.

"Maybe a bit about the French Impressionists," he admitted. "But I've read art books and sale catalogs and turned myself into an instant expert. You know my assignment, don't you?"

"No, what?" Mackie asked, liking him more.

"Buck Tolbert flies me to Rome, Paris, Amsterdam and everywhere—all expenses, the best hotels—to buy pictures. He wants two things, he told me: first, the works need to hold their investment value, and, second, every picture has to have a cow in it."

"A cow?"

"Buck likes cows. At first I thought, no, this is impossible, but then I found out that many of the major painters put an occasional cow in their works. It became a challenge. I went for it."

Mackie came out with her horse laugh.

"God, what a hell of a great laugh," he said, and they warmed to one another quickly after that. Two pretenders: delving into books, magazines, brochures and gossip columns by way of designing snooty jobs for themselves. Mackie wanted to tell him about Ray Bob's kisses, but held off.

While a Hungarian quartet soothed the teatime air with music, Don asked for her room number and seemed disappointed that she shared a big suite with the Browns.

"What kind of fun is that?" he asked, and she felt flattered.

Everybody ended up at the Criterion for dinner.

Mackie was being seated between Buck and Ray Bob, but Don boldly stopped that arrangement. "No, no, guys, I get the looker," he said, and with that he ushered her into a chair beside himself while the wives smiled with approval.

By the light of the oil lamps on the tables, Mackie knew she looked beautiful and that Don was turned on. She gobbled up the honey roasted pork, watched Don, and listened to Ray Bob and Buck shouting at each other at their adjoining seats.

"Lookee here," Ray Bob said, holding up a miniature croissant, "a little curved biscuit!"

Don sat quietly, grinning. His hair was an unruly coif:

messy, but somehow perfectly messy, and asking to be touched. In the taxi beside him, later, she resisted reaching out and running her blue fingernails through his hair, wondering if he might possibly be gay. He seemed manly enough with a down-home drawl, but arty, haughty rather than merely reserved, so who could say? As the evening ended at the elevators beyond the Ritz lobby, he seemed merely courteous and she felt a keen disappointment.

Hours later, unable to sleep, she called the concierge to complain that her room was chilly. The upper part of a window was open and she couldn't reach it, so cold air wafted in. Wrapping herself in one of the thick hotel robes, Mackie got into bed, covered up, and waited. Don Jacks kept stabbing into her thoughts: his mop of hair, his self-assurance, and the charming admission that he traveled all over the world buying expensive pictures of cows.

Eventually a plump concierge arrived with a battery of three young porters. Two of them carried armloads of firewood and went to work at the room's small grate. Another screwed together a length of metal pole, extended it, and closed the offending window. At last the concierge produced the single match that started Mackie's little fireplace and began his apology.

As they departed Mackie stood at the door, seeing them out. To her surprise she discovered Don Jacks, dressed in faded jeans, boots, and a golden cashmere sweater, waiting in the parlor of the suite. He raised a bottle of champagne in a silent salute as the porters filed out.

"I can't sleep either," he drawled, grinning. "And the door to your suite was open."

"Quiet or you'll wake up the Browns," she warned him, then she stepped aside, inviting him into her room. As she closed the door behind him they stood for a moment in the shadowy firelight.

"I didn't bring champagne glasses," he told her.

"Just put the bottle on the table," she instructed him, and she let the robe slide away to the floor as she turned back the coverlet and got into bed.

London filled up with the sweet ache of love: crisp late autumn days, taxi rides, plays in the West End, lunches at hip places, and nights together in bed. He was a slow, patient lover until his patience ran out and he became greedy as a cowboy, but she liked that part, too.

Ray Bob went without kisses for a few days. Meanwhile, Mackie worked on reservations at the Palace Hotel in St. Moritz and managed an invitation to a big party in Chelsea—for both the Browns and the Tolberts—where the American ambassador was a possible guest.

On a Saturday afternoon Don and Mackie walked along the embankment and found their way to the Savoy Chapel with its golden chancel.

"This is great," she said. "I want to say a prayer."

"For what?"

"Because we're here. I don't know what for."

Don stood in the shadows at the rear of the chapel while Mackie went down front, dropped to her knees, and gazed up at the emblems and cross in the stained glass window. She prayed "Now I lay me down to sleep," then a couple of old mealtime blessings, then fragments of a forgotten psalm. She felt dreadfully superficial and asked God if knowing you were superficial somehow made you less that way. She prayed for an orgasm with Don. She asked a blessing on all girl basketball players everywhere. She prayed that Ray Bob wouldn't want to kiss her anymore. She threw in a prayer for a little red car. Some tiny spiritual truth, she asked, give me just one. That orgasm, she prayed, let it come soon. When her knees hurt, she struggled to her feet.

They walked to Trafalgar holding hands and watching the sun filter through the last yellowing leaves.

As they stood hailing a taxi, Don asked her a question. "You think you can only be in love when you don't know the other person very well?" he wondered aloud as traffic flashed around them.

"Yeah, probably," Mackie answered, and she felt sad that this was true.

They were driven to a dealer in Soho Square who offered a 17th century Flemish tapestry with cows, dogs, sheep, peasants, and a prince on horseback. Don fingered the artwork, stepped back, squinted at it, pursed his lips, nodded, and finally pronounced it genuine. Then he studied the papers on its authenticity, reading them over carefully before turning to the dealer, a gaunt man dressed in funereal black.

"I like the tapestry, but these papers are a total fabrication," Don said, his voice dripping with arrogance and not a trace of a

Texas drawl. "My guess is that the former owner probably thought the tapestry was a fake and tried to bluff things through with all this stupid documentation. But the joke's on him. The tapestry's actually authentic and I'll pay your price without hesitation."

The dealer, impressed, swayed a bit as if struck across the cheek, while Mackie enjoyed Don's whole performance. Then while Don filled out a corporate check and delivery instructions, Mackie wandered through the rest of the establishment: antiques, paintings gone dark with age, just the right amount of stuffy British dust. She picked up a marble egg and pressed its coolness to her cheek, thinking about Don and his air of certainty: the last truly forceful man she had dated had been a linebacker.

In a taxi swerving back toward The Ritz he brought her fingers to his lips and kissed them.

"We've got to keep the Tolberts and the Browns together for a while," he whispered to her. "After skiing, we should sell them on Bermuda or some island paradise. I'm counting on you to arrange it."

"I'll sell them on something," she promised.

"My man Tolbert is trying to impress your man Brown with cow art and culture," he said with a short laugh. "But I worry that your boss will get tired of the bullshit and take you away. We can't have that."

He was almost saying he loved her. Mackie felt fevered—not unlike her childhood days back in Texas, out at White Rock Lake, when she used to break out in a heat rash. As he touched her leg she ran her blue fingernails through his mop of hair. Was this superficial or forever? Or was that the wrong question again and was this fever she felt part of some dreadful knowledge—locked away from her, sealed off from prayer, desperation, and her deepest longings? When in doubt, she decided, go with the flesh, and she opened herself to him, and the taxi driver was chatting on, and London was out there, permanent and proud, and he touched her like another beautiful tapestry, assuring her that she was genuine.

When she finally returned to the Browns' suite it was filled with shopping bags and packages.

"Sheila just about bought out a place called the Burlington Arcade," Ray Bob announced, grinning and somehow proud, and for a moment Mackie thought she might escape to her room, but didn't make it.

"You owe me four days of kisses," he went on, trying to sound lighthearted as he cut off her path. On the coffee table sat a large opened carton of chipped barbecue, the daily delivery. A shiny fork was stuck in it and a smear of sauce decorated Ray Bob's chin.

"I have some great ideas about the winter season," Mackie said, being evasive. "Places you'll really like."

"I talked with Sheila," he revealed. "She don't mind a bit if I buy a few kisses from you."

"Ray Bob, listen, the kissing is finished. There are no kisses on our winter agenda. Off the schedule altogether."

"It's that phony art expert, right? Let me tell you something about him. He goes around buying pictures of cows! And I have my suspicions if he's even from Texas!"

"He was raised in Odessa," she replied, and for good measure she threw in a creative lie. "Even played high school football!"

"Well, he's a hell of a distraction around here!"

"Good!" she shouted back, failing to notice that with a simple maneuver Ray Bob had backed her up to a sofa. "Good for me!"

"I'll bet he's getting more than kisses from you," Ray Bob said in a low growl, closing the distance between them.

"Whatever he's getting, it's free," Mackie hissed back.

They stood in an impasse, breathing hard, as Sheila came through the door with more shopping bags. "Know what? There's another arcade right down the street!" she called in greeting, and Mackie, relieved, gave the room her croaking laughter as Ray Bob stepped aside.

"What'd you buy?" Mackie asked, going to Sheila's side.

"Oh, nothing much, but poor old Buck's gonna have to take up fox hunting! Deva found this fancy sportsman's store and bought him a shotgun, a goddamned English saddle, and what all. What're you doin', Ray Bob? Trying to get the barbecue kissed off your mouth?"

"Goddammit, Sheila," he answered, and he went to a nearby window where he looked out into the gray mist and sulked.

"I've been trying to tell him about my winter plans for you guys," Mackie said, trying to sound cheery. "Saint Moritz, like we talked about, remember? Just to make the scene. Then lots of warm sunshine and beaches."

"Sounds good to me," Sheila replied, shedding her coat and kicking off her shoes. "And for Christ's sake let's take that handsome art buyer with us. He can keep you company 'cause I can't see Ray Bob and Buck throwin' their fat butts off a frozen mountain."

"I don't ski, I'm not goin' skiing, and I don't want to slog around some Santa village up in the goddamned Alps!" Ray Bob shouted from the window, and he definitely meant it, but Sheila just laughed and produced a Fendi handbag and a pair of matching shoes for Mackie's inspection.

"Are these kick ass or what?" Sheila asked, and Mackie gave the items her full admiration as Ray Bob disappeared.

At Saint Moritz the early season snow wasn't good, but Mackie had a busy first day. She moved them into the rented chalet: lots of glass and gray timbers, a servant and cook, a wine cellar, and rooms in the basement lined with all sizes of ski boots, skis, and clothing. She quickly arranged two parties for the Browns and Tolberts to attend: an African wildlife charity thing and a buffet hosted by an ex-dancer who had once done a specialty number in an old MGM musical. Mackie also briefed the cook on what to do with the daily barbecue delivery and taught Sheila and Deva how to get an English speaking operator on the phone. She rented a car and a snowmobile. She booked dinner at the Palace Hotel. Then she dressed herself in her new cobalt blue skiing outfit trimmed in fur, picked out a pair of blue ski boots downstairs, snapped on some parabolic skis, and hit the slope. She skied into town until the snow turned to slush in the street, then hoisted her skis on her shoulder and trudged to the Oldhaus, a tiny but expensive hotel where Don Jacks had insisted on rooms of his own. In the late afternoon of that first day she was deep in his thick goose down bed with him.

The room echoed with the slow tick of an antique mantle clock and the sound of sleigh bells that drifted in from the street below.

He told her that he had to go to Zurich.

"Not soon, I hope. When?"

"Tomorrow. Buck wants to put two paintings and the tapestry up for auction. He offered me ten percent of any profits we make, so I have to do it. But why don't we get away someplace together afterward?"

"Just say where."

"Maybe Spain. Help me decide. We've got to think over what's happening between us. I mean, where we go from here."

Heat rash time again. She felt her body begin to glow with that expectant and happy fever.

On the afternoon of the next day Sheila insisted that Mackie should join them in a little celebration back at the Palace Hotel. Although she missed Don and felt gloomy, Mackie agreed to go. In a small parlor adorned with red velvet and mahogany panels the Browns and the Tolberts drank champagne, then made a fuss about blindfolding Mackie.

"We have a present for you, Honey, so just go along with this," Sheila said, patting her, and with the blindfold in place they led her through the lobby and outside. She felt stupid, but went along with their enthusiasm until, finally, outside in the frosty cold, Ray Bob removed the blindfold and showed her the car: a red BMW convertible, shiny and new without so much as a single smudge of muddy snow on its spoked wheels.

"It's all yours," Ray Bob announced proudly.

"You deserve it, Honey," Sheila added.

Mackie knew immediately that she didn't deserve it at all, recalling her prayer back in that fancy chapel in London. Of all the things she prayed for, a little red car had been just a tidbit thrown in, not one of her more unselfish and serious pleas. So what did this mean? Was the prayer in all its parts going to be answered?

In spite of herself Mackie broke into tears. The Browns and the Tolberts loved this response although Mackie sobbed more with confusion than delight.

"There, there, Honey," Sheila consoled her. "Just hop in and take it for a spin! We want you happy! We want you bringing us to wonderful places like this for the rest of our lives!"

With that, they all lined up and kissed her on the cheek, although little muffin sized Buck almost had to climb her to do it.

That evening she spoke with Don on the phone. Static—a particularly bad connection—made his voice seem light years away. She learned that Buck Tolbert was sending him back to Amarillo to pick up a third painting for the Zurich auction.

"Then he wants me back in London at Sotheby's," Don told her. "It all makes sense financially, but if I didn't know better, I'd think Buck was trying to keep us apart."

"Ray Bob and Buck worked this out between them," she said, holding back the tears once more. Then she told him about the new car.

"We're both raking in the money right now," Don pointed out, being rational. "We'll get away together in a few weeks."

"Come to Bermuda right now," she said, and her voice broke.

"Right now I can make a killing and they're treating you like their long lost daughter. What color's the new car?"

"Red," she snapped at him. "And I don't want to be anybody's daughter!"

A week passed and part of another, then the Browns and the Tolberts packed up and went to Bermuda. Ray Bob shipped the car over, so Mackie took long drives around the island, stopping occasionally to stare at some picturesque cove and to let the wind muss her hair. For the first few nights she spoke with Don on the phone.

"They're trying to buy us off," she complained to him.

"No way that'll happen," he countered. "It won't be long before we see each other again."

"This guy hit on me today," she told him. "I was on the beach outside our villa eating a fish cake. This guy strolls over from next door and wants me to stay at his place—a salary and all expenses paid—while he goes on a business trip to South Africa. It turns out he's the local Daddy Warbucks. And seriously good looking."

"What are you saying?"

"Donny, we're going to meet other people. Time apart is deadly. We have to quit these jobs and get together!"

"We won't let money drive out love," he promised.

"So I'll quit this minute. How about you?"

He went on talking, not answering that. He wanted to make a million or two, he said, but time, she knew, would soon work its powers of erosion.

The next day she went snorkeling, driving both Ray Bob and Buck into a gawking frenzy even though she wore a simple black one piece suit. Face down over the coral reef, she stared at parrotfish swimming by, trying to clear her thoughts. That evening Don didn't phone. The next day she went with Sheila and Deva to the Yon-Ka Bodyworks, an upscale spa where their bodies were wrapped in seaweed then packed in steaming blankets. After the ordeal they went shopping, where Sheila bought Mackie a twelve

-place setting of Spode china, so many boxes that a spare room at the villa filled up with them. She decided to send the dishes to her Baptist mother and that made her stop and think about the Savoy Chapel and her prayer once again, and she wondered if the prayer of a wayward Baptist somehow became perverted there, so that one got little red cars as a kind of theological booby prize.

No phone calls that day, either. When he did phone he was at an airport without time to say much. His only endearment was, "We've got to get together," and it sounded like a cousin's offhanded message scrawled at the bottom of the yearly Christmas card.

A month went by in Bermuda's restless luxury and Mackie knew that she suffered some odd spiritual crisis, but she couldn't name it. The phone calls from Don ended. He was in Florence, maybe buying or selling the David.

The day came that the Browns were flying back to Dallas to buy a new house and the Tolberts were off to New York. Mackie had finished her packing when Ray Bob came into her room and closed the door behind him. He wanted to talk about Cabo San Lucas, the possible trip to Peru, this and that, but she insisted that all of that had been discussed with Sheila.

"So come to the point, Ray Bob, okay?" she finally said.

"I want to start up the kissing again," he said, and the words seemed to make him bold.

"C'mon, Ray Bob, we're done with that."

"Then kiss me for the BMW," he told her. "You owe me a kiss or two and you know it. The car was worth a thousand kisses. And never mind the clothes, the dishes for your mother, the salary, and what you gambled away here at the casino."

"Ray Bob, this is outright harassment."

"This is a goddamned business arrangement, pure and simple. Come over here and stand by me."

With a fixed smirk on her face, she obeyed. This won't go on forever, she told herself, and the car was worth plenty, the perks were extravagant, he was a fat old guy who would soon die from a coronary, money was brutal, and what the hell?

"That's better, Mackie," he said gently, tightening his hands around her waist. "Pucker up."

Her mouth trembled and she couldn't stop it, but she refused to cry or carry on. When you have a good job, she told herself,

you hang on. And I'm overpaid, way overpaid, and I'll do this
and think of Machu Picchu, of the far Pacific islands, of pillows
covered with satin, champagne and chocolates.

"I love you, you know," Ray Bob said under his breath.
"You're appreciated around here. And loved. I want you to
remember that. Now pucker up."

So she closed her eyes and did.

The Shadow That Lost Its Man

1

In the year before Mandela was released from prison and before all the political changes Cal went to South Africa to photograph a client in Johannesburg. His clients were still paying inflated prices for his portraits in those days so he traveled in style, staying at the best hotels and living, as he was fond of saying, single and superficial.

That morning it was The Carlton and he stood at the window of his suite gazing out at the skyscrapers of the city. His own face was mirrored there, too: a lean craggy face over forty years of age, no longer young, yet dark and handsome enough—with something of the predator about it—so that women seemed to know what he wanted and often gave it to him. He watched the street below his window—Wanderer's Street, a great name—and gave it his professional appraisal as if he meant to snap it with a wide-angle lens, then he looked at himself again and furniture of the room behind him: a layered effect, things superimposed, reflections on reflections. The city was like Dallas, where he grew up: generally clean, busy, and windblown. He felt energetic and confident in the way Americans, perhaps Texans in particular, often feel in foreign countries.

And he was certain that a new woman would show up.

One always did.

His client lived in Saxonwald, a suburb of bright garden estates beneath a canopy of eucalyptus and cottonwood trees. The villa was near the zoo, so occasionally a lion's muffled roar drifted in with the sounds of distant traffic and the clacking precision of all the lawn sprinklers.

Cal made his appearance in a yellow leather jacket and jeans, carrying his camera bags and presenting his business card. The card read, simply, Calvin Vega, and that said it all: portrait photographer, famous enough, expensive.

A little gray servant took the camera bags, set them inside the front door, and hurried away with the card. Eventually Cal was ushered through a portico and into a garden where General Hofmyr awaited him.

"Hello, my young friend," the General said, sweeping out his arm. "Can we do our work out here? This is my parade field these days. You like roses? How about an outdoor photograph?"

"My specialty is the close up," Cal answered. "But we can talk about it."

They shook hands as the General said, "Flowers and gardening clothes, that's my thought. So how long will this take?"

"If you're busy, I can come back."

"Oh no, very unbusy. Retired. My daughter arranged all this, you know. Says you want a dear price for it."

"I have two prices," Cal said, using an old line. "For work in focus and work out of focus. The pictures out of focus are called art, so they naturally cost more."

The General understood and laughed, placing his pruning shears on a stone wall.

"We're having lunch soon. My daughter instructed me to commandeer you for lunch. Hope it suits you."

"Sure, we'll use the afternoon light."

"And maybe you want to psychoanalyze me before you take my photo? To get the hidden self. Is that what you do?"

"No, none of that. We just pose you. And we discuss it, but in the end we do it my way."

"It's my face, but we do it your way?"

"You're only the subject."

"Like Picasso and his mistress, is it?"

"Exactly like that," Cal replied evenly.

His clients were wealthy, but their wealth varied. General Hofmyr was clearly one of the lesser clients and the fee for a portrait was perhaps something of a sacrifice. The villa was moderate in size, perhaps fifteen rooms with servants' quarters, pool house, and garden, but not without the need of paint and minor repairs. Oleander and roses camouflaged chipped masonry and missing tiles. The sitting rooms beyond the garden had a seedy look and their brass and silver lacked a military luster, so speculation became the game. Who wanted this portrait at fancy prices? Some organization? No, probably not, because few organizations would want to impress anybody with the Vega signature. Maybe the daughter? And, if so, why?

Before lunch they sat in a musty study overflowing with crowded bookshelves and stacks of dust-covered magazines. Occupying the space above the hearth was a 19th century oil painting of the battle of Blood River: Zulu warriors with their spears, Voortrekkers, cattle, wagons in a circle, brass cannon, an officer brandishing a pistol, and all the dead lying around a hippo pool in an eddy of the river. The painter had no particular talent, but the action had zest, a kind of B-movie breathlessness.

"Want your portrait with medals and braid and all that?"

"I've outgrown my uniforms," the old man grunted. "Besides, I fought with the British army in the real war. I've had nothing to do with these skirmishes in recent years—Angola and Caprivi and all that. Hell, I'm old. I knew Jan Smuts. I was a South African when we chose between Hitler and the Allies. There were supporters, you know, on both sides down here—at least until the madman marched into the Netherlands."

The General had a stubble of ashen beard, so needed a shave before sitting for his portrait. He was oddly soft and Cal had expected a baron with a swagger stick, something more severe, not this.

"I really don't know about politics," Cal admitted.

"Such a luxury, not to fret over politics!"

"Yes, but I suppose we should talk about posing for pictures instead."

"By all means. My daughter says to talk aesthetics—the ideas of photography, all that. She knows your reputation with women, I believe, from the magazines."

"The exaggerations of magazine writers have been good for my business," Cal allowed, shrugging.

"My daughter married a businessman who never liked me. They're divorced now, alimony and all that, and I think she wants my career on show for reasons of her own. As for me, well, I have a curious premonition about this portrait."

"A premonition?"

"Hmmm, a creepy feeling that it will somehow show me for what I am. Sounds crazy, I know."

"I hear this all the time," Cal assured him. "A lot of people fear that others will see secrets in their faces."

"Like kaffirs in the bush: don't want their photos snapped and their souls robbed. Yes, we've all heard that. Don't put any stock in it, do you?"

"Afraid not," Cal replied, smiling.

"Mind you, I'm not superstitious. I was an intuitive officer, but never superstitious. Yet I'm uneasy with this picture taking."

"You don't have to do it. You can tell your daughter that you didn't like me and won't have any of it."

"Oh, no, we'll go through with it. So my daughter can have her lunch with you. I think she wants to rub an ankle against your leg underneath the table. Just to check out your reputation."

"Is it time for lunch?"

"It is. Come on."

They walked through the portico into a room of high windows, skylights, and a table brightened with bowls of salad and shiny wine glasses with good silver.

"It isn't a premonition exactly," said the General, returning to the subject. "Tell me this, though: do you ever see in your photographs something that didn't seem to be there as you took the picture?"

Cal picked up an olive from a dish, ate it, then turned the wet seed in his fingers.

"I don't think about that sort of thing," he answered.

"But you're a professional. And, hm, take so many photos. You must've thought about it."

Cal smirked. "There have been a number of, oh, philosophers of photography," he said. "They usually ponder the obvious. Intellectuals. All intellectuals are usually, you know, intensely stupid. I mean, a photograph by its nature is superficial. And most of the so-called artists with the camera use the same technique: they take thousands of exposures, thousands, and only rarely will a picture have anything special about it. This afternoon I'll get you from dozens of angles and we'll hope one of them flatters you. That's all my work is."

"You don't much believe in your own craft."

"Belief has no part of it. I like photography without all the intellectual shit. And women who don't talk too much. And travel without, oh, you know, many destinations."

"Well argued, not that I believe you," the General told him.

"The camera lens is inferior to the human eye," Cal went on. "It doesn't actually see much. It distorts. It's too mechanical. Don't give it much credit."

He tossed the olive pit on the table: a casual gesture that somehow underscored his indifference. It landed beside a silver dish.

They turned to the sound of high heels on the patio.

"Ellen," said the General, greeting his daughter. She was a slender woman in her late thirties, blonde with a pageboy cut, wearing a silk dress and carrying an Italian handbag. Cal saw that she was probably one of those rare women who looked better naked than clothed, and she moved like liquid as if she knew this herself.

"You made a good choice," said the General during introductions. "I like your American photographer—although he doesn't believe in discussing the magic in his craft."

When she smiled at Cal for the first time he knew what was plainly there: she wanted a piece of him.

At lunch she asked direct questions.

"Have you ever been married?"

"Oh no, always a bachelor," he told her, and she covered that question with a flurry of conversation with her father.

He later caught her examining his face and hair, so she asked, "Do you go to women hairstylists or men?"

He waited a beat, then answered, "Women. And I like them to lean against me while they work."

She smiled and wanted more white wine, so the General summoned the little gray houseman who went searching for some. Her eyes flashed with mischief, as if she might be far ahead of what she actually said or did. Intelligent, Cal knew. Her eyes told on her.

"You published a book of nude studies," Ellen began once more. "Do you still photograph nudes?"

"Sure," he came back. "Wanta pose for me?"

The old man paid elaborate attention to his chicken salad.

"Possibly," she answered. "What do you have in mind? Something discreet or something for the girlie magazines?"

"You decide," Cal said, grinning, and the General snorted with laughter.

"I'd like something scandalous," said Ellen, her fork poised beside her face. "But pornography isn't really scandalous these days, is it?"

"No," Cal admitted. "But, damn, we could try."

She laughed out loud with her head thrown back. The curve of her neck, he decided, was hot enough by itself.

At the afternoon portrait session the old man wanted even more conversation, so had to be asked several times to sit quietly.

"Turn just so," Cal instructed him. "We want, you know, a Vermeer effect: the light put on without its source."

"See, you take technique very seriously," General Hofmyr noted.

"That's beside the point," Cal assured him. "This is just scrub work—like flying airplanes or driving busses. If it has any glamour or importance to anyone it's because I'm getting overpaid. Like that: the pilot makes more money than the bus driver, so he's more glamorous. There, keep your chin at that angle."

The General had been persuaded to wear a dark suit and tie, to sit indoors, and to allow his craggy face to become the featured object. He sat beside a window in good light. A mahogany chair and a pale tapestry were his props except for the book in his hand, a thin military memoir written long ago, his only written work, and it would remain or disappear as Cal decided how to crop the finished portrait.

"Do I look like a warrior?"

"Keep still," Cal replied, and he wanted to say, no, you look like somebody's gentle grandfather.

"You're very pragmatic and cynical, aren't you?" the General asked him. "But there's a school of thought that photography can be great—the same as paintings by the old masters."

"Sit quietly, please," Cal told him, smiling, and the old Hasselblad made its little noise.

2

They stood on Platform 16 waiting to board the Blue Train.

She had business at the Cape, she said, and asked him to come with her. It was a sexual dare, clearly, so he naturally said yes.

Like all the other women on the luxury train Ellen dressed in high heels, the Fendi scarf, the whole ta da, while Cal wore his jeans and leather jacket. She wouldn't look at him while they waited—as if she might break out in laughter if she did. He decided she was definitely hot, but loaded with karma: secrets and troubles he would never ask about.

Their compartment had fresh flowers and a chilled bottle of Cape wine. While he stuffed his photographic gear and bags into the top of the closet, she took off her shoes.

The train pulled out of the station's shadows into a bright and windy day. On the outskirts of the city he saw several yellowish mounds—each the size of a football stadium—and smelled the odor.

"Cyanide," she told him. "Residue from the old gold mines. They used tons of it to leach the gold away from the rock and now the wind carries the dust, everyone getting his nose and eyes burned, and everybody sort of, um, waiting around in the poison nowadays for things to get worse."

The skyscrapers became glints on the horizon and the veldt opened up: scrubby prairie like West Texas with low bushes and red clay fields littered with stones. A windmill passed, the only object in the flat landscape.

A short time later they sat in the dining car for lunch, awaiting the afternoon pleasures. He remembered a magazine assignment in South Africa years ago—his only other visit—when he went up to Kruger Park with a guide provided by the tourist board. Although he went to photograph the animals, the guide, Jill, posed for him openly and wantonly, giving herself to him in the VW van, in lodges, in tents, and on the lime grass beneath a thorn tree where a wandering lion might have strolled by to gobble them up in their distracted frenzy. Jill, yes: he wrote her name on the backs of the photos he made of her and some of them fell out of a book years later.

"What're you thinking about?" Ellen asked.

"My first visit here years ago. Kruger Park."

"I was wondering about the size of your cock."

"Adequate," he told her. "About the size of two beer cans."

She laughed and rolled a spoon around in her soup.

A soft underworld of women. He sometimes hired traveling companions, girls from the escort services, but usually he didn't have to. More often they appeared like this. Maybe something in his appraising glance turned them on, but who could say? Sexual communication was never a subtle business: a glance, a physical presence, recognitions learned by teenagers and occasionally perfected by a few devotees of the sport.

In his university days he fell in with the arty crowd. His photos were always girls and his pretentious friends called them nudes, wanting to see what he had in his darkroom, and he moved around the campus like a celebrity. Some of the early pictures appeared in his first published volume. The Vega signature. And his name became known and he was also Cal, Calvin, Cocky, darling, shugah, and names that came from strangers and less than strangers. The girls and their poses: girls whose gazes were pensive as poets and others, wide open and brazen, that might have resulted in his arrest.

In the dining car of the Blue Train he sat with Ellen, watching her watch him. She had a veneer of elegance about her and he recalled an Austin socialite who came on to him. She wanted a Rachmaninoff fuck, but he gave her "Night Train" instead, bracing her up against the wall of his darkroom while he took her from behind.

For a while he had money, mobility, and a career filled with assignments, but he was flippant about photography as art and described his work to a television interviewer as Lyric Titties. His pals laughed, but later a critic used it against him and if he conspired to condemn himself as a serious photographer he was satisfied when his work spiraled down into portrait work. He lived in New York, part of a group of young cockbirds and their girlfriends who gave their inebriated grins to Lincoln Center and the bistros. Portraits of the rich became his constant, the arty stuff all gone, and women became the currency he made and spent. He moved back to Texas, then to Malibu, then back to Texas again, and life was a series of projects, temporary alignments, and copulation or one of the several good substitutes. There was nothing pathological to it, he claimed, not at all, it was comedy, it was bachelorhood.

After coffee and a mint he and Ellen made their way back to their compartment. He set up a tripod because she wanted to play artist and model and he suspected she might want to play movie director in bed: go here, more of that, scenarios for every occasion.

"What's your business at the Cape?" he asked, removing her shoes.

"A party. Maybe more than one. And I want to, um, show you off. My social prize, do you mind? Also, I have a beach house at Clifton, so we can swim or lie around in the sand."

"Good, I'll photograph the ocean."

"The ocean needs attention," she agreed, smiling. "I'll undress myself now, if that's all right."

"Absolutely."

As she unbuttoned herself he slowly unbuckled his belt, pushed off his shoes, and slipped out of his jeans and briefs. Her eyes fixed on him.

She was far more beautiful without clothes: the rib cage and narrow waist. Large breasts with raised nipples. She stood and stretched, pulling her breasts high, then stepped out of her panties. Her mound wore a soft, light, delicate hair and not much of it: the cunt of a child, small and pouting.

She propped her legs apart on the couch.

"Want to photograph my ocean?" she asked.

3

He had seen Cape Town once before, those years ago, but it was better than he remember it: the great monolith of Table Mountain hovering over it, the crystal bay, flowers everywhere. A city perched on the edge of civilization: a space station brightly adorned on the dark continent. He had an impulse to take photos of it, but knew that would reduce its impact.

They took a taxi around Sea Point, then went on toward Clifton and a stretch of highway where, on their right, the villas clung to the cliffs below them. At one of these cliffside houses they turned through an arch and drove directly onto the rooftop parking space. As he paid the driver and gathered luggage, he heard seabirds wheeling and screeching overhead and could smell the soft rot of the salt breeze. The rooftop railings were sculpted with oleander and jacaranda. Beside their blossoms sat an old Jeep partially covered with tarpaulin.

"While I run my errands the next couple of days, that's your vehicle," Ellen said, pointing to it.

They made their way down a metal staircase into a house of white boxes and rectangles fitted into the rocky cliffside. The main room featured a wall of glass facing the ocean: a view miles out into the Atlantic. Books and magazines strewn around. Indian rugs and leather couches. A Tiffany lamp with a blue scarf draped over it. On a teakwood table beside a jade Buddha there was also a shiny 9mm pistol and a clip of bullets.

She caught him looking at it.

"There's a leopard in the neighborhood," she explained.

"A leopard? You're kidding."

She strolled into the kitchen, opened the blinds, and set out tumblers for drinks. "A few of the neighbors have actually, um, seen it. They say it's a big beautiful cat. It comes down from the mountain at night to raid the rubbish bins and occasionally it kills and eats a neighborhood pet."

Cal watched the afternoon sun catch her face in a nimbus of orange and she quickly returned his smile with her own. When he kissed her she leaned into him and opened her mouth.

"Let's play brother and sister," she suggested, whispering in his ear. "I'm fifteen years old and you're just fourteen. Our parents are drunks and never know anything. Every night I come to your room."

They found their way to a wide leather chair.

"Come on, little brother, hurry," she whispered, urging him.

Maybe she'd used this fantasy before, whispering in someone else's ear, but he didn't care. While she moved with an oiled grace she kept whispering, telling the story, acting her part, instructing him, and he went with it.

The restaurant, later, was called Blue: a candlelit spot on the hillside above the Cape highway. As they finished a bottle of wine after the meal, Cal brought up the subject of the troubles. He mentioned it casually, not really knowing the players: tribal leaders, churchmen, politicians, Brits or Afrikaners.

"Um, no, please, not tonight," Ellen responded. "Tonight there's no slum called Crossroads, no secret police, no tribes, just us. But I will tell you about the poet bomber."

"Oh? And who's that?"

"Nobody knows who he is. But he rigs his bombs in high places on crowded streets, so that his couplets explode and come raining down. According to his literary critics, he writes fair iambic pentameter. Last week a blast of poetry went off at the top of a flagpole in Longmarket Street. Shattered a few windows."

"And the police can't catch him?"

"No, bloody grand, isn't it? He just composes a few, um, revolutionary verses and mixes in the right amount of explosives. No one ever gets hurt—at least not so far."

"A guy could get killed with a poetry grenade," Cal offered.

"Ah, but to die for one's art and craft!" she said with mock awe, and they had a laugh.

Back at the cliffside house she strolled into the bedroom, shedding her clothes as she went.

"All right, you're the gardener and very, um, dirty. Your fingernails are black and you smell of fertilizer and sweat. You asked to come into the house for a drink of water, but I want a bit more than that and I'll pay you extra."

She perched herself on the thick pillows at the head of the bed and he walked on his knees across the coverlet to join her. He loved playing the gardener. And Ellen loved it so much that he began to feel like a witness rather than the participant.

Later they lay in each other's arms and when he told her how beautiful she was she said, no, not really, my mother was very beautiful, but I've only been a bit pretty. He asked if she had a brother and the question made her laugh.

"A brother? Oh no, that was just our little game! I didn't actually have a brother!"

He asked about her father instead.

"He's an old dear," she offered. "But he never liked my friends or any of my opinions. He was a traditional military hero, you see, with lots of medals. But that was years ago. World War Two. Everyone knew him and he could've stood for office, I suppose, and served in Pretoria and all that. And the portrait, well, I want it to remind people who he was, of course, and on the selfish side I want to, um, be thought of as the General's daughter. Is that bad of me?"

"Not at all," he assured her.

"So. Do you take many photos of fashion models?"

"What brings that to mind?"

"Making photos, all that."

"Sometimes in the past, yes, I've done fashion sessions."

"I think models are so sad. Beautiful and sad."

"Sure, I guess so," he agreed.

"Beauty is a curse, you realize," she said, sighing. "My mother spent her life being beautiful. And sometimes I think places are cursed with their beauty, too. As if, um, the beautiful places on earth have a way of turning us into fools and fanatics. Like Bavaria with all its lovely forests and mountains somehow had a part in making the Third Reich happen. You think I'm right in this?"

"Sure, maybe," he replied. "But men also fight over ugly, worthless pieces of ground, too, don't they?"

"They do, yes," she agreed, turning against him so that their breath mingled. "But a beautiful homeland makes feelings run so deep. The territorial thing. A South African farmer can think of his land and get tears in his eyes."

"Are you that way, too?"

"I love my country. And it's dreadfully beautiful and so—well, so deceptive and troublesome."

Ending the reverie, she smiled and kissed his nose. Then she closed her eyes and drifted toward sleep. Propped on an elbow, he lay there watching her, feeling a peaceful rapture with this good humored, intelligent, and wanton woman. In the morning, he though, I'll call my answering service in the States, but I won't go back just yet.

4

He slept ten hours that night and when he awoke she had left him a note saying that her errands would be finished by noon. The note lay beneath the keys to the old Jeep.

Instead of calling his service or looking for a darkroom for rent—the General's portrait could wait, he decided—he drove the Jeep to an open café near Bantry Bay, where he had breakfast, then drove to Sea Point and strolled around the sea wall. Young white surfers and their girlfriends lolled on the beach drinking beer, their vague eyes straying off toward the breakers. Under a concrete bridge two boys—a surly white and a smirking Indian, both maybe eleven years old—smoked a joint and gave him a hard glance as he passed. An old black couple, arm in arm, prosperous, balanced their ice cream cones as they sauntered along the row of palm trees.

A newspaper kiosk had a copy of *Texas Monthly*—a small South African surprise—so he bought it along with the newspapers.

It was more than an hour before noon when he drove back to Ellen's, parked on the roof, and made his way back down the winding stairs into the house. He turned the key in the lock and entered the main room.

A man in a light brown suit stood beside the coffee table.

"Hello," said the stranger, turning. "And who are you?"

"A friend of Ellen's," Cal answered. "Who're you and how'd you get in?"

"Take it easy. I'm Tom Steyn. Here, see, I've got a key, too."

"Ellen's not here," Cal told him.

"Right, she's not. And you're, ah, what? The new boy-friend?"

"Cal Vega," Cal answered, crossing to the coffee table and dropping his magazine and newspapers there. The pistol, he noted, was absent and a brown envelope occupied the table.

"That's for Ellen," Steyn said, gesturing toward the envelope. "I just came by to drop it off. American, are you? With a Texas accent, I believe."

Cal nodded. The tell-tale magazine lay between them, so Steyn was observant and quick. He was also a big man, red-faced with a heavy mustache. When he grinned, the broken capillaries in his face became radiant. He spoke with a deep Afrikaner baritone and resembled a singer in a barbershop quartet, yet there was a certain menace and authority to him.

"How do you like our country?"

"Love it. This is my second visit. I was here years ago."

"Ah, you come here on business?"

"I'm a portrait photographer. I just did Ellen's father in Johannesburg."

"Ah sure, and how's the General?"

"I'm sure you keep up with him."

"Actually, I've been working almost exclusively with Ellen, but I can't anymore. The packet explains that. Lovely here at the Cape this time of year, don't you agree?"

"Very pretty."

"You should take the drive down to Cape Point. The flowers are all in bloom. You should go, really. We're at our best just now. The troubles in our country, they just fade away at this time of year. Fade away. We have things in hand, you know."

Cal couldn't determine what was wrong. Steyn was perhaps three inches over six feet, maybe two hundred and fifty pounds, florid and out of shape, yet wore his khaki suit like a tailored uniform. Was he one of Ellen's lovers? God, Cal thought, she must have dozens.

"I'd like to visit with Ellen, but I can't stay," Steyn went on. "Tell her I stopped off to leave the packet. Cal Vega, is it? Is that a Mexican name?" He smiled and those capillaries in his cheeks became a crimson blotch. Betrayed, Cal decided, by a blush. Steyn was uncomfortable, but hiding it as best as he could.

"My father was Mexican and my mother Irish."

"Ah, I see. Now Texas: that's a place I'd like to visit. The Houston Space Center. Cowboys. JR's ranch in Dallas. Or is that just a show on the telly?"

"Just a show," Cal answered, knowing that Steyn knew this very well. At the door they shook hands and said their goodbyes.

Afterward Cal strolled back to the coffee table and stared at the envelope. It was sealed, but he wanted to open it.

Finally he sat down with the newspapers and magazine. Who was that guy? He saw in the *Cape Times* that the poet bomber had struck again: a loud and harmless blast in a mall. Glass everywhere, but no injuries. The poetry, translated from the Afrikaans for English speaking reader, was filled with lines like *the stem of nightshade erupts into morning*, a sort of sophomoric Zen warrior earnestness.

The old issue of *Texas Monthly* brought back a few memories: chicken fried steak at Threadgill's, a pal named Chigger, Shiner and Lone Star, Rosa's Tex-Mex, and the drawling humor. After a time he put the magazine aside and gazed out on his Atlantic vista. For better or worse, he knew, he was much the same: scoring, dodging, moving on through a landscape of assorted snapshots without theme. He wished Ellen would come back for a long afternoon rut.

She soon pushed through the door with a bag of groceries. Cal took the bag from her arms, kissed her, and followed her into the kitchen.

"You went out too," she said. "You have today's newspapers."

Her voice was light and airy and she seemed glad to see him.

"Yeah, and your poet bomber is loose again."

"I heard about it. In the shopping mall."

She put items away in the kitchen as he told her, "There was a guy in the house when I came back. Said he has his own key. Tom Steyn. He left an envelope for you."

"Oh?" she replied casually as she worked.

"Big guy. Said he was a friend."

She turned to him with a smile that somehow failed. "Where's the envelope?" she asked, and it was more important than she wanted him to detect.

"In there on the table," he replied, trying to ignore her secrets. For an instant he felt surprised at himself for wanting to know her better.

She strolled into the main room, picked up the envelope, thought about it, then didn't open it. Instead she came back to him and put her arms around his neck. "Let's play masseuse," she said in a husky growl, nuzzling him.

They opened the windows, letting the ocean's sounds and salty odors drift indoors. She undressed him slowly, then peeled out of her own clothes. Placing him in their favorite chair again, she stood behind him and gave him a slow facial: her fingers moving lightly over his eyes, forehead, and mouth.

"Relax," she whispered. "I'm your masseuse making her weekly house call. Your wife is always here in the house, watching, and until now we haven't had sex. But today she's gone. So I undressed, too. And let you watch my little striptease. And now we're alone. So relax."

"Sorry," he told her, grinning. "Impossible."

"My beautiful dark client needs professional help. He needs release from all his worries."

The rubdown evolved. After a time she wedged into the chair beside him and after sex Cal stretched out on the floor wondering if some real masseur had done her. He also wondered about the guy in the business suit with the mysterious envelope, but warned himself, no, what the hell, why do I want to know her secrets? I won't ask.

She stood at the window looking out to sea, pushing her hair off her neck, posing for him, then she said, "Let's drive down to Danger Point and stay with Enid at the ranch. The party's down there tomorrow, but we should go early. She'll love it if we just show up."

"Who's Enid?"

"An old family friend. Let's do it. We'll have lunch on the way.

And we'll wear jeans. Nothing fancy for the next two days."

She came over and pulled him to his feet, then kissed him.

He was playing by Ellen's rules, but didn't care.

5

In the old Jeep they drove out the N1 toward the northeast, turning into the coastal mountains. Old Huguenot villages appeared along with pastel fields of wildflowers. A fish eagle sailed over an orchard of trees heavy with blossoms. In the foothills the houses grew larger and more severe: an elegance of rich farms and emerald vineyards. With its Dutch Cape architecture each house wore its white-faced gables like bibs: prim starched pilgrims standing up straight and pious in the landscape. Landed wealth: a foreign, curious phenomenon to Cal, and something that stirred up a vague hostility in him.

They passed a white church in an arbor of giant oaks. In the shadow of its steeple stood a cluster of believers decked out in dark suits and silk dresses for a wedding or funeral. The sturdy bourgeois: children in their arms, the seasons ticking in their veins, labor and harvest in their stubborn theologies. Not his sort. He knew them as sanctimonious bastards with pride, dirt, and savings accounts. No trespassers allowed. Play it straight or keep out. Under the eye of the camera, he knew, their faces turned to milk and nothingness.

Rolling green foothills arrived, then valley after valley of lush vineyards: the grapevines neatly staked, the rows clean, all of it aglow in sunlight. A warm January day, the middle of the Cape summer.

He and Ellen talked about Enid, who had once, long ago, been her father's mistress. "Watch out," she warned him. "Enid's a hell of a flirt. Old as she is. She has this big place on the sea: a ranch with, um, horses, cats, books, videos, art, and rusted farm implements."

She turned to catch him looking into her denim shirt. "Hey, give it a rest," she said, and she gave him her slutty laugh.

They drove into a high grassland of electric green, mountain cliffs all around them.

"Before I was born there were Cape lions in these mountains," she said, driving. "But they became extinct, so I never saw one. Yet I miss them. Sounds ridiculous, I know, but it's so sad."

Wistful and somehow far away, Ellen had a wild, curious strength—a thing he somehow knew, but couldn't put into words.

On a road high above the sea as they turned eastward there stood a pile of smooth stones fashioned into a crude shrine. It bore a wooden sign with hand-painted words: The Church of the New Zion. Standing beside it was a gnarled black man with a Bible in one hand and an umbrella in the other, an umbrella decorated with bright plastic strips, bangles, and pictures cut from faded magazines.

"*Muti,*" Ellen remarked as they passed. "A medicine man and his little roadside church."

"What's he got? A magic umbrella?"

"If it keeps the rain off him with all those holes in it, it would be a miraculous umbrella," she answered, smiling.

They entered a gated ranch: high grass, views of the sea, horses in the fields.

"Did you bring your camera?" she asked.

"Sure," he said. "With strangers I hide behind cameras."

The house appeared, an unexpected and oversized igloo: a white scoop of ice cream melting on the green landscape. As they approached he leaned out the window and made two quick exposures.

Enid met them on the lawn, sweeping out to greet them. She was full of affectations and lots of *dahlings*, but Cal liked her. They managed introductions, admiring each other's clothing.

"Leather—and a nice yellow," she said, stroking his jacket, and her breathy voice trailed off into a guttural sound, an amused growl.

The interior of her house was an extravagance of curves: no straight walls, the corners rounded, the doorways swept up in plaster arches, balconies curving out to offer sea views. Enid herself was costumed in a Lagerfeld jacket, red, with tight jeans and an assortment of beads.

"Oh god, sit down! Please, dahlings, anywhere! Let's get drunk! What a season this as been! Half the horses decided to get sick!"

This spouting, of course, was a cover, and Ellen dutifully rolled her eyes and acknowledged it with laughter. As Enid poured out the gin in reckless measurements, she assessed Cal and he knew that her observations were shutter-speed quick. As she stirred up drinks, he stepped back, raised his camera, and clicked off shots of the room, the two women, and the balcony views. Enid seemed to love him for it.

"Yes, Dear, please, take it all in! This house is a curative for everyone's ills! Don't you feel it? Here, sit beside me. Where'd you find this creature, Ellen? God, look at the thighs on this beast!"

They drank and laughed at her performance. He made another exposure. Everything was white with splashes of color— done with a designer's care. On the table beside their tumblers of gin was a Tarot deck.

The old woman started immediately on her dead husbands. "I knew they were doomed, dahlings, not that I wanted them to go, but they were all elderly, don't you see? Although I didn't marry a single one of them for his money, no, I'm not that sort, I married strictly for love each time and nursed them all to the bloody end!"

"You wore them out," Ellen commented.

"Sexually, you mean? Well, mind you, I never refused any of them, but if I helped them toward their graves with a bit of sexual exercise it was their own lewd gluttony, nothing more or less."

"Enid was a sex machine," Ellen said, grinning. "Her husbands always left their calm and ladylike wives for her, though, so, yes, it was, um, their own damn fault."

"Now, Cal, believe this, dahling, death has an aura about it," Enid said more solemnly. "It gets in the air before it actually happens. As though the ghost gets all restless inside the body!"

"Don't go mystical," Ellen told her, smirking.

"I can't help it, dahling! Death is quite moving. I mean, I was holding Terry's hand. That's the first husband, the one in the export business—which is to say he bought and sold anything that moved through the shipping lanes of this world. Trinkets. Shiploads of stolen refrigerators. Bananas. Once he bought the entire pineapple crop of Zambia. Another time he had these six lorries filled with fertilizer moving all over Africa from one country to the next. They started out for Kampala, but he had a better offer in Kenya, so directed them there. Then Lusaka phoned, so he switched again. Spent all his profit on petrol being wonderfully indecisive!"

"You were holding his hand?" Cal prompted her.

"Oh, dahling, yes, the life went out of him and I felt it go.

He became a husk and I held this hand, this empty hand, and he was quite gone. What are you anyway? A Scorpio, I'll wager."

"Good guess," Cal admitted.

"Not a guess at all. I'm psychic—especially around dark good looking men."

"She's coming on to you," Ellen warned him.

"Of course, naturally! We should get drunk and take a nice bath together, how about it?"

"I'm going riding," Ellen announced, laughing and rising.

"Oh, see, he's a definite Scorpio!" Enid said, grabbing Cal's hand. "And your lifeline, dahling, goes all the way around your wrist! And look at that heartline! Oh, you cruel bastard! Ellen, look, he's going to pull your heart out of your pretty chest!"

"He already has. And I'm going to find myself a mount while there's still a bit of daylight."

"Take the gray and don't fall off," Enid instructed her. "You've had a nice stiff gin, you remember!"

When Ellen departed, Enid sat back and smiled at Cal. She was seventy, perhaps a great deal more: thin lipped, hawk-like, with a nervous charm that quickly settled into seriousness as it did now.

"Now, dahling, don't you want me to tell your fortune?"

"I'm not a believer," he assured her.

"Ah, yes, I can see that. And I could use your palm or the Tarot, but all that's just mechanism. I can see a great deal without any of that. For instance, on the way here you passed *yurt*—a little shelter, the church of the Muti."

"It's there on the road," he said, grinning. "You know very well that we passed by it."

"Yes, but you felt something as you passed. A stirring. You had this emotion you don't understand and, well, dahling, the Muti brought it forward in you, didn't he?"

Cal sipped his gin, not denying it. But how, he wondered, did she know this?

"Tell me about Ellen," he urged her, changing the subject.

"Ah, such a love. Won't she tell you about herself?"

"Not really," he admitted.

"So there's only sex between you?"

Cal shrugged. That was enough, he wanted to say. Yet it wasn't.

"She's very special to many of us," Enid offered. "She's our courage. Can I explain this to you? You're not political in the least, are you?"

"Back home I vote Democrat," he said, smiling.

"There, yes, quite so. Americans and their politics. In the rest of the world the activists take risks, bleed, and often go crazy for politics. Unfortunately, perhaps, we're all in that category here, dahling, and can't help ourselves. It's too much sex, too much wine, and too many strong passions for us. And difficult for you to comprehend, I'd wager."

He sipped his gin, listening.

"You're intrigued with her," Enid continued. "Of course you are, dahling, and no wonder. Her lovers undoubtedly feel—well, her depth. They detect it, yet few of them know exactly what it is. For that matter I don't fully understand her myself and I've known her since her childhood. She was always stronger than the rest of us. And fearless. We admire her and we want to be fearless, too, although we just can't."

He kept his silence until Enid said, "I'll make a prediction: when your time with her is finished, you'll be someone else entirely."

"That's true of all affairs," he offered, trying a little worldly wisdom of his own.

"Hmmm, yes, true, but now you are going to find what we call the *onverwacht*, the unexpected. It's everywhere for you now. It surrounds you. And that's what you're feeling."

That evening a cool rain arrived, so Enid asked Cal to build up a fire in the hearth. The women set out cold cuts, opened several bottles of wine, and filled his ears with gossip. They spoke openly about how, after Ellen's mother died, the General carried on with Enid for a while. They ended it, Enid said, because General Hofmyr couldn't afford her and because she was too mystical for him.

"So how did you two get to know each other?" Cal asked.

"When Ellen was little, dahling, we had our conspiracies against her father. In those days it was toys and treats, but later on it was political. The General has always been too stuffy for us."

"Also, Enid would talk sex with me," Ellen added. "And, after all, the national sport of South Africa isn't rugby. It's copulation."

"Highest divorce rate in the world and we're proud of it," Enid said. "And we pride ourselves in knowing exactly who's fucking who, don't we, Ellen, my dear?"

"We're a small and talkative little tribe," Ellen admitted. "And we also talk openly about sex because we usually can't mention the really important matter of race. When that subject comes up we have to speak in codes and follow all sorts of social courtesies. So what's the dinner topic going to be? Sexual chitchat. And it's always fashionable to have something on the side—and to talk about it within limits. Because there's this great lie hanging around. We have to be candid about our lesser sins."

"Now don't get started, my dear," Enid warned.

"Right. We'll concentrate of tomorrow's party. Is everyone coming?"

"So far as I know," Enid replied. "Including Moppo. Talk about your handsome black man!"

"Oh, do me a great favor, Cal, please. Take lots of photos," Ellen said, touching his sleeve. "Will you? Just be our official photographer? Please?"

"Like group snapshots?"

"If you don't mind."

"Sure. What's the celebration?"

"Just friends getting together," Ellen assured him. "Another party. We do lots of parties because, um, these days you never know."

6

That night in their bedroom Ellen wanted more games.

They played schoolmaster and student.

She reported to his office—the little writing desk in the alcove beside their bed—wearing cotton knee stockings, a short pleated skirt, and a white blouse primly buttoned up. She submitted to punishment for breaking school rules, so he sat her on his lap and gave the upturned palms of her hands a few gentle slaps. Then she stripped down to the knee stockings and asked to receive the rod that her schoolmates had told her so much about.

In all this he was the stern schoolmaster, not Cal.

She smiled and laughed, yet had a faraway look in her eyes, too, as if the fantasy was everything.

Cal tried to keep up with all her instructions. "Bite me," she insisted. "I've been a bad girl and I deserve a rough fuck."

Later they played a threesome with his camera.

"Pretend it's a movie camera," she began. I'm the porno

queen and you're the cinematographer. You always watch me with the hired studs, but tonight there's a snowstorm and you offer to drive me home. We're in Stockholm. And we go to my flat and I ask if you want to fuck me and you say, yes, sure, but you also want to film whatever we do. So there, hm, do that in slow motion. Perfect. Are you filming? Slow, slow motion, ah, freeze frame, good, now slow motion again."

When they finished he stretched out on the bed, groaning.

"No more," he complained. "You've used me up."

"There's a great silence in the Stockholm winter," she said drowsily. "The silence plays with your head. Then, sometimes, the sound of a distant teacup brings you back. You return to your normal and complicated awareness. Know what I mean?"

"Hm," he replied.

Later he asked why she had commissioned her father's portrait.

"It's a long story."

"Tell me," he said, knowing she didn't really want to.

"In my teen years I was this raging liberal," she began, sighing.

"And you irritated him."

"Very. Many demonstrations and petitions. I was also dating interracial. The General wasn't for apartheid, not at all, but when I dated black guys, he went a little bonkers. I had to become very secretive because of him. Now it suits me to have myself identified with his military career and his more conservative views. I'd like to present the portrait to his old regiment someday soon—and to have my own photo in the newspapers doing it."

"Then the portrait's really for you?"

"Absolutely," she admitted. "The General's far too modest and too tight with his money to want such a thing for himself. Here now, are you really too tired out?"

He assured her he was.

"I'll give you an hour. Take a nap. Then I want some middle-of-the-night attention."

As she nestled in the crook of his arm he groaned again.

7

The next day around noon the guests arrived, more than twenty of them in several vehicles.

Ellen greeted each one: a tall black woman, eight black men, an old Indian gentlemen, the rest whites. She also kept signaling to Cal to take photographs of everyone in groups of three or four. All the while she introduced him as her famous American photographer and one of the Brits, Neville, professed to know Cal's work.

They smiled and posed for his camera, yet they were a somber group, academics wearing earnest expressions and whispering in small clusters around the house and terraces. Enid circulated with a tray of drinks—dahlings! hello!—but couldn't stir up a party mood.

Ellen moved from one group to another, too, touching everyone, smiling, and joining their discussions. As she moved around, she energized them: nods, guarded laughter occasionally, then bursts of renewed conversation. Cal saw a new Ellen: the hostess, clearly, and in some curious way the centerpiece of the occasion. Ellen and the tall black women exchanged fierce hugs and kissed each other's cheeks. Later, Cal went over and introduced himself for the second time. The woman had big hair, a tight red dress, and spiked heels that put her two inches taller than Cal. One of her gold ear bangles was held together by a delicate strip of soiled adhesive tape.

Maybe, he decided, she's from some escort service. A fine ass on a willowy frame. He decided to hit on her, lightly.

"Ever been on the Blue Train?" he asked, starting up.

"No, not really. The Blue Train's for diplomats and such."

"But suppose I bought tickets and you came along as my personal secretary?" he suggested.

She gave him a smirk and a throaty laugh. "If I traveled on the Blue Train I'd call attention to myself," she answered. "Even if I was in your hire, they might detain me. And my papers aren't in such good order, so anything could happen."

"Because of the pass laws? Would it be illegal, then?"

"Ah, screw illegal. I don't mind illegal. Even my skin is bloody illegal, isn't it?"

"So if I paid you well you might risk it?"

"I might. In a posh hotel or nightclub nobody says anything about a white tourist and his black escort, so the Blue Train might be like that. You're a cheeky sort. Are you actually asking me to go?"

"Not at the moment. What's your name?"

"Pola. I work in water resources.

"Good," he said, smiling.

The afternoon, after lunch, eased into a soft inebriation so that the groups seemed less intense and more friendly. Cal, satisfied that a single roll of 35mm film was enough, stopped taking pictures and drank, in turn, a nice Riesling, some grappa, and a bit of pike brandy. Then he met Moppo, clearly an important figure in the group: the only black wine master in the region, he learned, and a remarkable physical specimen. Moppo had a muscled, easy grace with a thin waist, wide shoulders, and biceps straining against his short sleeves. His hands were twice the size of Cal's, rough and black with grey calluses and shiny pink nails. His shirt was Ralph Lauren denim and he wore jeans and snakeskin boots, so he looked like a prosperous Texas rancher, a man of the soil no longer required to work it with his own strength. Cal listened while Moppo told how his workers had recently removed the stones from the fields, giant stones used to reflect the sun's heat in the cooler months so the grapes would ripen faster. He heard, too, how the Petrus was added in a certain amount to the Loudenne this year to achieve the Merlot and how, in Moppo's opinion, this would be a vintage year because of the right amounts of rain, dew, and sun. A boring, technical sort of man, cal decided, trying to impress others with his station in life.

Around the house before supper the talk ranged from something called Wits to Helena Bonham-Carter to AIDS among the mineworkers.

Neville, the Brit, tended to make speeches. "Eighty years ago we were a beloved people throughout the world," he said, once. His listeners consisted of Pola and the old Indian—who might have been deaf. "President Kruger was welcomed in Europe as if he's established a paradise," he went on. "General Jan Smuts was the spiritual father of the League of Nations—and wrote, in fact, the bloody preamble to the charter of the UN. We had moral leadership! And it was our belief in fairness and coexistence that started us off!"

Cal excused himself, moved away, and found Enid.

"Dahling! Having a good time?"

"These are serious people," he complained.

"So true. And they improve very little as they get drunk."

"Where's Ellen?"

Enid couldn't say. As he looked for her, he stopped for a cup of espresso with Pola.

They talked for a while and she told him a story.

"When I was a girl in the Christian school some police came with their fiber glass quirts," she said, turning the coffee cup in her long fingers. "They whipped two of our teachers in the hallway. One of my schoolmates threw a stone at their lorry, so they also beat her. When someone is hit by a quirt, ah, it makes a white streak on the black sin, then the white streak opens up, it sort of flowers, it opens like this, and the blood comes out."

"This is your elementary school?"

"I was, ah, twelve years old. One of the policemen questioned me about my political beliefs. He took his quirt and raised the front of my dress with it while he did this."

Cal fell silent.

"Yes, I was once a very good Zulu girl in the Christian school in Durban. I even attended one year at University. But, ah, no scholarship and too many boyfriends. That year I went to demonstrations and then, well, to say the truth, I became afraid. Our friends were in detention. But you don't want to hear all this."

He assured her that he did, yet didn't. Eventually he moved away where Moppo stopped him. He wanted his photograph with his new truck, so Cal found his camera and they went outdoors. In the last light of day Moppo posed with his snakeskin boot on the bumper of a shiny Dodge Ram.

At supper they toasted names Cal didn't know: many toasts, some of them tearful, so that he knew these were people no longer with them. Toward midnight Ellen led him up to their bedroom. She slipped out of her jeans—no panties—and asked if he had taken photos of everybody.

"I just shot one roll—thirty-six exposures—but, yeah, I got everybody and several of Moppo and his new truck."

"I appreciate it, Cal, really, but do me a favor, will you?"

"You're doing me one right now," he said, admiring her.

"Like it?"

"Love it. What's the favor?"

"Keep the roll of film and give it to me later back in Cape Town."

"Sure. And c'mere," he said, grinning.

She strolled toward him, but remained less playful than he expected. "Something else," she said. "I can't drive back with you. I'll come, um, a day later. And if you don't mind, love, would you check into a hotel instead of going back to my place?"

Let her have her intrigue, he decided. Maybe someone else was on her dance card. "I'll check into the Mount Nelson," he offered. "When do you think you'll join me?"

"Why don't we say lunch day after tomorrow?"

He assumed she did have someone else, possibly the guy who showed up in her place or somebody here at the party. He wondered ever so briefly if Pola might be available.

"Sounds good," he replied. "Lunchtime in two days. Anything else?"

"Oh, I hope so," she said, finally crawling onto the bed and once more propping herself on a mound of pillows. She summoned him with a crooked finger.

"Tell you what," he said, undressing and joining her. "Why don't we play Cal and Ellen this time?"

"We did that on the train. Let's do jailbait instead."

"Jailbait?" he asked, manufacturing a smile and moving against her. He covered his disappointment by kissing her shoulder.

"You're the warden and I'm your prisoner. You demand favors of me while I'm wearing handcuffs," she said, and she arched herself and held her hands above her head.

Although he submitted, he felt annoyed.

On the train, he clearly remembered, they had played artist and model.

8

Cal was assigned to drive back to Cape Town with the talkative Brit, Neville, who started right away on Americans.

"Naturally, Americans have heard of South Africa and its problems, but then all news and information is much the same to them. It comes over the telly, gets a nod, then on to the next item. Michael Jackson's sex: now there's a burning issue. Or what Marlon or Liz or some randy politician is doing. The world's real horrors sort of blend into the show biz. Americans are a loud and trivial people, as trivial as rock music."

Cal slumped in anger, watching the passing scenery and trying to think of some clever retort, but managed only, "Everybody's happy to have us as the world's policemen. When there's dirty work everyone wants the Yanks to go clean it up, right?"

"Yes, but Americans are like tourists for the most part," Neville went on. "They wander in and out of countries taking culture samples. They're nomads. The passing caravan. They never actually understand or feel anyone else's problems, do they? They just want the world to behave itself—and they believe they can throw money at people's difference and make everything jolly."

They drove on the N1, traffic whizzing by. Neville's Toyota had the odor of leather and pipe tobacco.

After a few more miles, though, Neville revealed his true discontent. "I suppose you're shagging Ellen?" he asked with as much fake indifference as he could muster.

"Oh, sure," Cal replied casually, then he allowed the silence to gather between them. "Actually, Neville, she loves Americans. We fuck like cowboys. At least I do."

It was the meanest thing he could imagine to say.

9

Cal's window at the Mount Nelson Hotel had views of Lion's Head and the edge of Table Mountain, then, from another angle, the sunny waters of the South Atlantic.

He spent the next day on the telephone with his widowed mother, his answering service, his broker, and the secretary of a prospective client in Atlanta, but after the telephone voices ended a gnawing loneliness set in. He wanted Ellen's body and presence and although he was scheduled to fly back to the States he wanted to stay. He cursed himself for coming back to the city without her, for not knowing about her friends or business, and for not even knowing Enid's last name—although, of course, Enid had worn several last names, never mind which one the phone company might currently have listed at Danger Point.

He paced around the hotel room. Her lovers, Enid had said, using the plural. And her courage. What did he know about Ellen except her abandon in bed? And wasn't that enough—and the sum of what had been between them? When she went into orgasm she raised her head slightly, then slammed it back onto the pillow. They used each other like narcotics. Bang away and thanks. Good sex and goodbye. Yet the old satisfactions somehow weren't enough and an unnamed yearning kept washing over him.

Danger Point. He wasn't even sure where the hell it was.

137

In the afternoon he took a walk around the hotel's grounds and garden, then strolled downhill through the Botanical Gardens to the city. He picked up a newspaper, but tossed it away, unread, in a wire basket. He wondered if she'd consider flying back to the States with him. He thought about all her games. Little brother. The silent snow of Stockholm.

He slept badly that night, waking for long periods. A fierce wind came up, laying siege to the hotel. He imagined the ocean out there: giant whitecaps in a black night.

The next morning, tired and distracted, he had coffee in his room, then made early lunch plans hoping Ellen would soon arrive. He paced around thinking about entrapments. If I'm a little obsessed with her, he told himself, I should be careful.

Just after ten o'clock that morning he stood at his window in his shirt and shorts, one sock on, when the phone rang.

Neville's voice was cold and brittle.

"Don't say my name on the phone," Neville instructed him. "This must be very quick, but you need to know. Ellen's dead. So is Enid. So is Moppo and Pola. A car crash last night east of Brensmark."

Cal sat down heavily on the windowsill.

"The report," Neville went on, his voice breaking. "The report is that their bodies burned up in the crash. But that's always the story to avoid autopsies, isn't it? That's always the convenient lie they tell."

"Who do you mean?" Cal managed.

"Who do I mean? The death squads. Who the hell do you think I mean, you dumb prick?"

10

Cal rented a car, bought an elaborate road map, and started driving into the wine country toward a small town called Brensmark. Although he didn't fully understand why, he meant to hurry to the site of the wreck. Inside him was a cold shadow, a new presence that took away most rational thought.

The narrow mountain highway beyond Stellenbosch twisted through a series of dark glades, a shadowland where even in the bright summer day a blue pall settled in the valleys. The inhabitants of the glades—viewed from his car window as he slowed down in the turns—were light-skinned and mysterious, a people in the no-man's land of a mixed race, and for Cal, he felt, the glades bore some of the atmosphere of the Deep South in America, the scraggly byways and stopovers of, say, Tennessee or Kentucky where smoke and mist settle in the low spots and where thin dogs lurk beside rusted junkyards, ramshackle houses and leaning barns. Occasionally the curves of the road opened up into wider meadows, and set back in stands of timber or alongside rocky streams Cal glimpsed large stone houses or another gabled farm mansion, never exactly elegant, where some landowner in his winery or farm looked out over his feudal domain. The scattered hovels, he knew, belonged to farm workers—farms replete with those scrawny, long-legged chickens pecking in the dust, those inedible looking birds common over the whole continent. The hovels said clearly, look, poor folks here: water spigots in the yards, no screens on the windows, sad mules, work, Jesus, and early death.

Then arcades of overhanging boughs blotted out the sun as he drove by forests of pine and hardwood that turned the day to quicksilver. In the hairpin turns he stole quick glances into that netherworld of shadowed glades, and it became his own little horror movie: the dark wood, down and down.

He passed through the sleepy little Huguenot town of Brensmark, then kept going east. Not far away at the edge of another forest the burned out husk of the Jeep lay against a tree off the shoulder of the road, its front bashed in, its doors open like charred wings. An immense cottonwood tree nearby sent out its airy white particles on the afternoon breeze, adorning the blackened roof of the vehicle.

Cal parked beside a road flare. A uniformed policeman waved traffic around the scene.

Taking his little Minox out of his gear, Cal walked toward the wreckage. Out of the forest came two men, the largest of them with a walkie-talkie, waving, and calling, "Hold on, please! No photos!"

Cal kept walking toward the wreck until both men intercepted him. Both were tailored khaki suits, not unlike the one worn by Steyn, the man Cal had met at Ellen's cliffside house.

"You from a newspaper?" the big man barked at him.

"No, just curious," Cal answered.

"Then put your camera away and move on! No photographs!"

The remains of the Jeep sat in a circle of scorched ground. Seeing it, Cal fought for control. The searing heat, he kept thinking. Her body burned up, gone. He trudged back to his rented car as those delicate white particles from the cottonwood settled on him in penitent silence.

As he put his camera away, a Mercedes limo pulled up. A young army sergeant quickly jumped out to open the rear door with a salute, then, slowly, the old man emerged: General Hofmyr, somehow older, wearing his green garden smock and rubber boots. He saw the wreckage immediately, then hurriedly looked away, focusing his gaze on the treetops.

Cal made his way toward the group that formed: the General, his driver, the two men in khaki, the traffic cop. Introductions and information were exchanged before he reached them, then the old man raised his eyes to Cal.

"The portrait photographer," Cal added after offering his name, and the General looked at him absently, struggling for recognition, then finally shook his head.

"Yes, oh yes," the old man said with a rasp. "Yes, my boy. And we won't be needing that picture now, will we?" With that he turned and shuffled toward the wreckage.

The acknowledgement, though, allowed Cal to linger and he joined the others. The burnt Jeep seemed at rest against the trunk of an old oak tree, its chassis charred, yet undented. The left front fender and bumper were missing. The rear tires were flat and the petrol tank had blown, so that an explosion and fire had obviously originated at the rear of the vehicle. The seats had been removed with the occupants. A sickening odor stayed on: petrol and—what? Cal didn't want to think about it.

Those white cottonwood particles floated down.

The old General shuffled slowly around the wreckage, his eyes clear and observant. He knew. And he spoke to himself softly, his voice dry and feeble, although Cal moved close enough to overhear.

"I told her," he said in a soft rasp. "I told her a thousand times."

11

Once, lying in bed together, not more than a week ago, Cal remembered, Ellen talked about the wildflowers.

When the Ice Age descended millions of years ago, she said, moving down the polar cap to cover Europe in its flow, slicing the Alps into Matterhorns then freezing northern Africa in its onslaught, the Cape was spared. Because the Ice Age didn't reach this far south, she explained, five thousand species of flora were saved and the tip of the continent became a kingdom of wildflowers unlike anyplace on earth.

Now she was buried on a hillside in view of a rich canopy of growth that dazzled the countryside; the foothills of the coastal mountains had turned to flame for her and the meadows became bright embers in the morning sunrise. Around the gravesite tall red blooms moved like trembling fingers in the slight breeze, so that Cal asked a young black woman standing nearby what they were called. Wild Watsonia. From his vantage point Cal could view both the mountains and sea: a white beach lay like the crook of a shining arm, holding back the surf, and in a faraway crease of the mountains a cluster of slate covered roofs presented themselves to the hazy sunlight.

He estimated the crowd at the funeral at more than three thousand, mostly blacks, mostly young, with dozens of those grim faced men in tailored khaki suits—the security force—moving through and around the cemetery.

He saw no one he recognized from Enid's party: not Neville, not the old Indian gentleman, no one.

Hunched over in the only chair beside the casket, the old General looked small and beaten.

A leader of the Reformed Church, a portly white man in a robe trimmed with crimson, offered a long prayer, then an old black woman surrounded by girls in berets who raised their clenched fists, spoke at length, saying, once, "With so many whites we were always standing at the gate, but with Ellen we were always home and inside the house straightaway!" While the crowd responded with amens, a young man with a thick cowlick of blond hair stepped up and tried to lead a song, but his voice broke and the girls in berets picked up the tune and came to his rescue.

Cal watched as that cold shadow stirred inside him. He thought of yesterday's newspaper where some friend of the family had been quoted as saying that police versions of the accident were "probably true." In a competing newspaper there was no mention of either the accident or the funeral arrangements, not even a modest obituary.

After an hour he moved with the crowd toward the bottom of the hill, wildflowers all around them, then a dusty road opened up, a road lined with cars, old busses, and a few rickety lorries. In that silent file of mourners Cal saw Tom Steyn and moved toward him, pushing through until he was close enough to call out.

"Can you talk with me?" Cal pleaded as they were jostled by the crowd.

"About what?" Steyn replied, although once again he blushed red. He knew.

"Please," said Cal, and he held onto Steyn's sleeve until at last the man relented.

"Yes, all right, I'll come to your hotel," Steyn told him.

"Do you know which hotel?"

"Of course. Four o'clock today in the bar. That suit you?"

Cal thanked him as the movement of the crowd separated them again. For a moment he stood by himself, mourners passing by. The sun bore down on his shoulders as his shadow was thrown with those around him, and he felt that he was merely shadow now, nothing more, and the shadow was deep inside him.

12

"I'll not contact you again after this, Mr. Vega, and if you make an effort to contact me I'll avoid you. Officially, you could be a great bother to everyone. It isn't personal with me. On the contrary. I'll tell others that you're an American tourist pestering a detective about a delicate matter—and that he's a very busy man who hasn't time for you. Understand?"

Cal nodded. They sat in a secluded booth of dark wood while a lone waiter stood across the room talking on the telephone.

Steyn's crimson blush came and went, making Cal wonder if this coloring served as a kind of lie detector.

"This was entirely a security matter," Steyn went on, heaving a sigh. "The case is now closed and will never be reopened. The bodies, as you probably know, were cremated after being badly burned in the wreck. There was no autopsy and no medical report beyond that. There's a one page traffic report on the accident, nothing more."

They turned their drinks in their hands.

"You knew her only for a short time, Mr. Vega, and you

didn't know her very well. I understand you met her up in Jo'burg while working on a portrait of her father, then came down here with her on the Blue Train—sharing the same compartment. Cruel as this might sound, she probably had some use for you. I've personally known the General for many years. His father and my father and all that. And I've know Ellen most of her life. She was someone you fancied you were using for sex, I'll wager, but I don't want to presume. In truth, she was a clever woman who never made a move without a practical and political motive."

"I loved Ellen," Cal insisted.

"No you didn't," said the detective with a short, harsh laugh.

As the man flushed red at this assertion, they both sipped their drinks.

"There's the Civil Cooperation Bureau," Steyn began again. "You've probably never heard of it. It's a secret army unit. And Ellen and her friends ranked high on their annoyance list."

"You sound as though you don't really care for them," Cal ventured.

"We all hate the bloody fuckers, but there they are. But see here, Mr. Vega, we're a nation of informants, aren't we? We're worse than the Irish in that way. Spying and telling on one another. Since somebody's probably watching us right this minute, I'll have to file a report by way of covering myself, don't you see? And if later you repeat anything I've said to you in confidence I'll turn against you. I'll say you're a bloody liar. Because I'm a family man. Two children. My father worked most of his life as a mine guard and we were poor. And if my job often shows me the worst of this country I'm still a proud professional, believe me, and I hate murder or seeing anyone get away with it."

Cal believed him.

"I was a friend to Ellen and tried to help. That packet I left at her house that day we first met, well, it was a bit of information I tried to provide. Information and a warning, Mr. Vega, because I knew the danger."

The detective gazed around the empty bar as the color gathered in his cheeks. He was trying hard to be patient with Cal.

"If someone in this country ever advocates violence," he went on, "they're considered a terrorist, no two ways about it. And we want our terrorists dead—same as you—as a matter of convenience. When you turn on your tap, you don't care where the water comes from. When you switch on your telly, you don't want to know the physics of it. You just want things to work. Convenient like. Same as we do, you Americans want your terrorists and criminals out of sight, preferably dead. But cold-blooded murder sticks in the throat no matter who does it. Even if the state does it, it's bloody business, so take my advice: buy yourself an airline ticket and leave. Then try to live with circumstances."

Cal nodded and finished his whiskey.

"You didn't know her," Steyn went on. "She was dangerous and you should've been afraid. Me, I'm afraid all the time. Because accidents can happen to any of us. Even having this little conversation with you has its risks and could present me with a whole set of bloody damned problems."

Although the detective spoke quietly he had turned crimson.

"By the way, those photos you made for Ellen," he went on. "You didn't give them to Neville or anyone else, did you?"

"No, they're here in my pocket. The undeveloped roll."

"They're meant for me. Will you please let me have them?"

Cal hesitated.

"Ellen was looking for the informant at her party. I was the one who would inspect the photos and hope to tell her the informant's identity. Of course it's already too late for her and the others, but I might save somebody else's life if I can make an identification."

Cal handed over the roll of film. "I suppose I have to trust you," he said.

They both slid out of the booth. The detective managed a grim smile. "Please, Mr. Vega. You're a long way from Texas. You're on my turf. I know what I'm telling you. Go home."

13

The midsummer heat of Austin.

From the window of his studio in the hill country just west of the city Cal watched his mother squinting beneath a wide straw hat as she watered the rose bushes and sipped iced tea. Her absent gaze was far away, so the hard stream from the hose splashed a hole beside one of her favorite bushes. His mother stayed with him for a few weeks, moving around in her distracted way, more feeble than he liked to think about, yet she gave him companionship and something to occupy his thoughts when he wasn't working.

He had just come back from doing a portrait in Atlanta. His subject, a society woman, exuded a fake effervescence, and was the sort of woman he called formerly cute.

While in Atlanta he picked up another woman, a divorcee with a deep sunburn who worked with men in hardhats on a road crew. In his hotel room, stripped for his inspection, her arms and face were bright red while the rest of her body gave off a sad, pale glow. They fumbled around on the bed until he asked her to leave, making her so angry that he thought they might have a fistfight.

His efforts, recently, had become comedy without laughter.

Now he stood in a blast of noonday heat on his deck. He drank a salty dog. To the west lay the rocky Texas hill country. It reminded him of the flatland viewed from the windows of the Blue Train and had become his own little arid karoo. When he looked out on it these days—he had come back from South Africa more than a year ago—he felt that shadow inside him, a presence nobody else could possibly know about or detect.

South Africa, of course, was in every newscast: Mandela released from prison, the pass laws abolished, so much. It was history, detached and unreal, the abstractions of politics, yet the private history down inside his own sad darkroom of the self, that hurt: Ellen's face and body, the curve of her breast as it sloped away from her underarm, her sly glance, her slutty laughter. He missed her, missed the man he once was, and had somehow missed, he knew, a great chance in his life, so that he felt dull and stupid. I was stupid, he told himself: stupid, stupid, stupid.

CPSIA information can be obtained
at www.ICGtesting.com
Printed in the USA
LVHW040842300123
738071LV00001B/9